BLUE PAINTS

Rabbit's first impulse was to attack the man, to fight to the death in defense of this important amulet of the People. Good judgment restrained him. If he were killed, there would be no one to retrieve the all-important medicine object. No one would even know where to look. Even so, he must protest.

"It is an evil thing you do," he warned.

"The evil falls on you," the other laughed.

The warriors were finished plundering his camp, and their chief turned away. Rabbit was so certain that they intended to kill him that he was prepared when the terse command came.

Rabbit, though he understood not a word of the strangers' tongue, was certain of the meaning.

"Kill him!"

Rabbit started to turn at a sound behind him. From the corner of his eye he glimpsed a descending weapon. He tried to dodge, but too late.

The war club struck a glancing blow above his ear, and his senses exploded like the crash of real-fire in the Moon of Thunder. Then there was blackness. . . .

**MOON OF THUNDER
by
Don Coldsmith**

Bantam books by Don Coldsmith.
Ask your bookseller for the books you have missed.

Moon of Thunder

》》 》》 》》 》》 》》 》》 》》 》》 》》 》》

DON COLDSMITH

BANTAM BOOKS
TORONTO · NEW YORK · LONDON · SYDNEY · AUCKLAND

All of the characters in this book
are fictitious, and any resemblance
to actual persons, living or dead,
is purely coincidental.

RL 6, IL age 12 and up

*This edition contains the complete text
of the original hardcover edition.*
NOT ONE WORD HAS BEEN OMITTED.

MOON OF THUNDER

*A Bantam Book / published by arrangement with
Doubleday*

PRINTING HISTORY
*Doubleday edition published January 1985
Bantam edition / August 1988*

Introduction
by Dale L. Walker
》》 》

Don Coldsmith's Spanish Bit novels are tales of horses as much as men: the horse is not only the pervasive symbol in the books but is, by the purposeful design of the author, the heart of the Saga.

This is as it should be. The author, in electing to write of life among native American tribes of the sixteenth or seventeenth centuries, those People just then touched by the advent in their lands of Spanish explorers, chose this time and place in history carefully and perceptively. A seemingly tranquil, even uneventful time two centuries before Lewis and Clark set out from St. Louis to follow the Missouri into Indian lands, Coldsmith's setting was in fact an era and place of cataclysmic change. And no factor of that process of change quite matched the introduction among the People of the Spanish horse.

How this fateful animal altered "Indian" civilization once and for all time, is Coldsmith's theme throughout the Spanish Bit Saga. It is a noble theme constructed around a noble animal and here, in the seventh book of the Saga, there is no lessening of the pervasive presence of that compelling, history-making beast.

vi >> INTRODUCTION

In *Moon of Thunder*, when Rabbit, son of the medicine
man Owl of the Elk-dog clan of the People, rides out
from his tribe's camp in search of his vision quest, the
new century has just dawned. The events of the novel
occur in about the year 1600, nearly six decades after
Juan Garcia, a young officer in Coronado's expedition
into the trackless reaches of New Spain, became lost,
encountered members of the tribe known as the People,
and took the name given him when he first removed his
Conquistador's helmet—Heads Off.

Heads Off, in the years to follow his momentous ven-
ture into their lands astride a strange animal as large as
an elk and doing the work of a dog, rises to lead the
Elk-dog band and his horse's ornate Spanish bit becomes
a tribal talisman, a revered object of great medicine.

Rabbit, aged sixteen winters, is the grandson of Heads
Off and he begins his vision quest during the Moon of
Thunder, riding out from his people's Turkey Creek camp
toward a flat-topped finger of land jutting over a river
valley not too distant from home. Entrusted to him is
the sacred Spanish bit and the stallion Gray Cloud, among
the finest horses of his clan—an animal whose bloodline
is traced to the first Elk-dog, that which Heads Off rose
into their lands some sixty winters ago.

As times passes from the advent of Heads Off among the
People, the changes in the migrations, daily lives and
habits of Rabbit's clan and all the neighboring clans, even
the warring and antagonistic clans (such as that old enemy of the Elk-dogs, the Head-Splitters, and Rabbit's
new nemesis, the Blue Paints) are all the result of the
changes brought about by the introduction of the horse
to their culture.

When Rabbit is rescued during his vision quest by
Yellow Bird of the River People, we learn what the horse
culture has meant to her tribe. The River folk are no
longer content to grow corn and pumpkins, but now
pursue the buffalo—on horseback. Within the space of a
few seasons, the River People have moved away from the
watercourses into the plains, following the buffalo herds,
moving their skin lodges from place to place and successfully competing as hunters for a place on the prairies.

It is a peculiar fact of history that while in the valleys
of Mexico, the highlands of South America and the jun-

gles of Central America, great civilizations flourished centuries before the first Europeans visited the "New World," no such empires and civilizations were known to that vast, immensely rich territory that came to be known as the United States. There, until the sixteenth century, a million people lived in varying degrees of primitivism—weavers, fisher folk, farmers using tools of stone and wood, hunters using stone-headed weapons to kill their game and to brain their enemies. The lives of these people were essentially static with even the most nomadic of them wandering but short distances from established tribal grounds.

These First Americans had several fatal deficiencies in common, chief among them a lack of knowledge of making tools and weapons from the metals found in abundance all around them, and the fact that they had no horses.

Wild horses were indigenous to North America and ancient Indian tribes killed them for food tens of thousands of years before the first Europeans set foot upon the continent. But, for reasons yet unknown, the native American horse disappeared about 15,000 years ago.

Columbus brought the first domesticated horses—used for transportation and as pack animals—to the West Indies in 1493, and Hernando Cortes brought the first—a mere sixteen head in all—to the North American continent in 1519. Spanish exploring expeditions such as those of Panfilo de Narvaez in 1528 and Hernando de Soto in 1539, introduced the horse to Florida and Georgia and expeditions, including those of Francisco Vasquez de Coronado in 1540 and Juan de Onate in 1595, brought their horses to the American Southwest.

The great Spirit horse of Rabbit's vision quest in *Moon of Thunder* is the leader of a band of mustangs (an English corruption of the Spanish word "mesteno," an un-branded animal claimed by the "Mesta," a Spanish stockman's association) descended from the horses brought to the New World in the era of conquest—perhaps from strays from Coronado's expedition in search of the Seven Cities of Cibola.

Coronado, governor of New Galicia, the northwest province of New Spain, was twenty-nine when he set forth in search of Cibola on February 23, 1540 with 300 soldiers,

a number of Indian guides and about 1,000 horses. After
five months of arduous travel at the head of an advance
column of his force, Coronado reached the Indian city of
legend—a place that turned out to be no more than a
collection of humble Zuni huts. Pushing westward the
following year on the trail of yet another supposed city of
gold, grandly called Quivira, Coronado and his men made
their way to the Rio Grande, crossed the Pecos and Brazos
rivers, roamed into present-day Oklahoma, crossed the
Canadian River and the Arkansas and turned northeast
into Kansas, traveling northeast to the Kansas River and
finally reached Quivira, an even bigger disappointment
than Cibola—a modest camp of Wichita Indians.

Coronado led his dispirited force, reduced by death,
privation and desertion to about 100 men, back to New
Spain. He had found no fabulous cities and no gold, but
his men had discovered the Colorado River and the Grand
Canyon, had blazed a trail from Mexico to Kansas, and
had recorded for the first time the cultures of the natives
they had encountered.

They also, in all likelihood, left stray horses in their
wake.

The advent of the horse into the primitive society of
the People of Don Coldsmith's Saga may be said to have
been the beginning of the end of their stone-age society.
When Juan Garcia first saw the band of the People he
was destined to dwell among and lead for the rest of his
life, he found a tribe which had yet to discover the
wheel, had yet to discover metals and their uses, a tribe
which, for all its wisdom, lived not far above the cave-
dwellers at the dawn of man.

Above all other gifts, the horse gave the People mobility. It enabled them to move and carry their lodgings and
goods with them as they sought better camps with more
abundant game, water, and better weather. The horse
made hunting game as prized (but formidable) as the
buffalo possible on a large, organized and regular scale.
The horse made it feasible to continue the hunt when
game close to home had been thinned. The horse made it
possible for the intermixing of the clans (and of warring
among them as often as friendly contact) and tribes for
the powerful confederation of those far-flung (by stan-
dards of foot travel) tribes and clans.

The horse gave the People mobility and such concomitant gifts (the product of the horseback hunt) as food, clothing and lodging. The horse, in brief, gave the People knowledge, wealth and power.

It is easy to lose oneself in Don Coldsmith's narrations of life among the People in these simple times and such is the quiet power of his story-telling that the reader may lose sight of the fact that the world elsewhere also continued to change.

Contrasting the life and culture of the People with what was occurring in the rest of the world at the time of the events in *Moon of Thunder* is in fact a startling example of historical parallel.

In the same year Rabbit rode out of his tribe's camp toward that finger of land:

—William Shakespeare's "As You Like It" ("All the world's a stage./And all the men and women merely players"), "The Merry Wives of Windsor," and "Julius Caesar" were written;

—The Honorable East India Company was chartered to make voyages to the Indies via the Cape of Good Hope to compete with the Dutch in the spice trade;

—The French established a fur-trade colony on the St. Lawrence River;

—The most populous nation in Europe was France with 16 million people (compared to about 10 million in Spain and Portugal and 5 million in England);

—Only three years had passed since Galileo invented the draftsman's compass, a device which will serve for centuries to solve algebraic problems;

—Only three years remained in the life of Elizabeth I (whose death will mark the end of a 118-year Tudor reign in England) and in the lives of 33,000 Londoners who will die in the plague known as the Black Death.

Such was the stage and some of the players of the rest of the world at the time of the events of *Moon of Thunder*.

The horse, while not alone among "civilizing" influences brought to the People by outsiders, was a potent force in changing their lives for all time and this is Don Coldsmith's compelling lesson as the Spanish Bit Saga continues to unfold.

1

>> >> >>

Drizzling rain pattered down on the camp of the
People. Fat, greasy drops drummed on the sodden skin
lodge covers and dribbled downward in rivulets that became waterfalls at the skins' edges.

It was the Moon of Thunder, and the weather had been
warm and dry. The People had left the Sun Dance and
Big Council, and the Elk-dog band had camped here on
Turkey Creek for the summer. The heat had become
oppressive, and lodge covers were raised, like lifted skirts,
to allow the breezes to circulate.

The formation of towering thunderclouds to the west
had been a welcome sight. The People sat in the shelter
of the lifted lodge covers and watched the deliberate
approach of Rain Maker. He marched relentlessly toward
them across the distant prairie, occasionally striking with
his spears of real-fire and sounding the booming thunder
of his dance drum.

Some of the more timid scurried around, untying and
lowering lodge covers to peg them tightly to the ground.
But to most, the cooling shift in the wind, and the prom-
ise of refreshing rain, was a welcome change. They sat

1

watching the storm from under the raised lodge covers
and calling cheerfully to each other as it approached.

It was a gentle rain, washing the dust from the prairie
to release the glorious damp smells that a summer shower
brings.

Rabbit sat in the lodge of his father and watched the
drops bounce on the skins of the adjacent shelter. He had
much to think about in this, his seventeenth summer. It
was assumed by the entire band that he would follow in
the footsteps of his father, Owl. He had no objection to
this. He rather enjoyed the special prestige he experienced as the son of the medicine man and grandson of
Heads Off, one of the band chiefs of the People.

Yet, Rabbit had been a restless youth. Partly, he was
certain, it was that he felt a special responsibility. He
was the youngest and the only surviving male in the
family line in this generation. He could barely remember
the death of his cousin, Bobcat, as a young man. It had
been a time of much mourning. There was much talk
when Eagle Woman, sister of Bobcat, assumed warrior
status in his stead. She was now called simply Running
Eagle, one of few women in the band to wear a mascu-
line name not modified by the term "Woman." Rabbit
admired her greatly.

But now, he felt that he must prove his worth to
uphold his position and that of the family. Eventually he
would be a medicine man, and a good one, but first he
wished recognition as a hunter and warrior.

Already he had proved his skill at the hunt. Now he felt
that he was ready to seek his vision quest. Perhaps that
would improve his status. Possibly, even, he could outgrow
his name. Rabbit. It was a childish name, one given by
childhood friends when they had noticed his slightly
prominent teeth. The name had stuck, and through the
seasons he had come to find it increasingly distasteful.
Rabbit longed for a deed of valor which would earn for him
a dignified name, one a warrior would be proud to wear.

"Your thoughts are far away, my son."

It was a statement, not a question, as Owl smoked and
relaxed against his willow backrest.

Rabbit's mother glanced up from her cooking. She had
noticed the young man's frustration. She picked up another smooth cooking stone from the fire with her tongs

and dropped it into the rawhide-lined pit. There was a sharp hissing sound from the bubbling stew, and fragrant steam rose in a puff.

Willow turned attention again to her son, who had not yet answered his father's implied question. Rabbit drew a long breath and exhaled audibly. Then he spoke, not really directly to either of his parents. To the world at large, perhaps. Or, more likely, to himself.

"It is time to seek my vision."

His father nodded, almost imperceptibly. Owl was pleased. No one could tell another when the time was right for his vision quest, but the signs had recently pointed to it. Rabbit was restless, almost inattentive in his apprenticeship to his father's medicine. Owl puffed his pipe a little longer, and when there was no further conversation from Rabbit, the older man spoke again.

"When will you go?"

"When the storm is over."

Owl nodded assent. The Moon of Thunder was characterized on the plains by good, sometimes even glorious weather. During the pleasant, sunny days that seemed to belie the name of the Moon, it was good to travel, to hunt, to take advantage of the excellent climate. It was a good time for a vision quest.

The summer storms which gave the season its name would sweep across the prairie and wash it clean. Then, before Rain Maker's next onslaught, there would be several suns of pleasant, comfortable weather. They would provide an uninterrupted few days' fasting and far-seeing, without distraction. Surely this would be a time for seeking meaningful visions.

Rabbit had already chosen the place for his quest. It was a high, flat-topped finger of land jutting over a river valley. On three sides, there was a precipitous drop to the grassy meadows and tree-fringed stream below. On the fourth side, the narrow strip of level upland widened very gradually into the endless sweep of the tallgrass prairie. From the very tip of the fingerlike bluff, one could see for more than a day's travel in any direction. The green of rolling hills blended into the blue-green of the next ridge and the even bluer one beyond that. Rabbit had always been fascinated by the different shades of blue, becoming more indistinct in the distance until the

last line of hills could hardly be distinguished from the
blue of the sky itself. It was to this spot that he would go
for his vision quest.

The rain had nearly stopped now, and Rabbit rose.

"I will leave in the morning."

His father nodded again. He rose and knocked the
dottle from his pipe.

"It is good. Come, we will look after the horses."

"Not too long! The food is almost ready!" Willow
called after them.

She knew that her two men might need a little time
together to silently share their feelings of this important
event in Rabbit's life. The horses were only an excuse to
be together a little while.

Aiee, how empty the lodge would seem! Willow had
barely adjusted to the emptiness when their daughter
Red Bird and her husband had moved out to establish
their own lodge. She did not relish the day when Rabbit
would find a wife and move to the lodge of her parents.
At least he had selected no one yet.

Willow took her tongs and added another cooking stone
to the stew, watching the fluid bubble up again. It seemed
only yesterday that Rabbit was born, after years of trying for
a second child. Now he was grown, ready to seek his vision.

How like his father the young man was. She remembered her first meeting with Owl, when he had been no
older than this. They had both been prisoners of the
Head Splitters. Young Owl had seemed so thoughtful, so
sensitive, that she had been attracted to him immediately.
It was more than the fact that they were of the same
tribe, prisoners of the enemy.

She recalled their childish, furtive courtship and their
disastrous attempt to escape. Still, the spirits had finally
smiled on them, and they had been able to return to the
People. Now, in their son Rabbit, Willow saw much of
the shy thoughtfulness of his father at the same age. He
would be an able medicine man when the time came.
But the time was not yet. Rabbit had unfinished thoughts
of his own to resolve before he became ready. His vision
quest would be of much help.

She could hear sound of the men returning and turned
to stir the cooking meat. She must feed Rabbit well if his
fast would begin tomorrow.

2

》 》 》

Rabbit slept little that night. The clouds that formed
the trailing edge of Rain Maker's tattered robe broke up
into smaller rags and dispersed, leaving the sky clear at
day's end. The young man lay on his bed of robes to the
right of the doorway and watched the slow circle of the
stars around the Real-star. A night bird called somewhere, and the musical trill of a toad's song was followed
by the hollow cry of *Kookooskoos*, the great owl.

It seemed an eternity before the gray of the false dawn
began to pale the eastern sky. Rabbit rose and went
outside impatiently. It was still some time before the
first rays of Sun Boy's torch flickered over earth's rim
and the People began to stir.

The mists of the night still hung heavily over the
stream as Rabbit embraced his parents and threaded his
way among the lodges of the band to begin his vision
quest. He stopped a moment at the lodge of his grandpar-
ents. The hair of the band chief was snowy white now
and had been since Rabbit could remember. Heads Off,
past sixty winters, still carried himself well, his back
stiff as an arrow. His most remarkable feature, however,

was a full growth of fur upon his face. It, too, was snowy white.

Rabbit had grown up with the vague understanding that his grandfather had come from another tribe where all men had fur upon their faces. He was unsure about the women. Both Rabbit's father and Eagle, his uncle, had some facial fur. Even Rabbit himself showed a dark fringe along the upper lip.

Somehow, he had come to believe that the possession of facial hair was connected with the medicine of elk-dogs. At least, it was told, the People had had no horses at all until the coming of Heads Off. The young outsider had brought the first elk-dog they had ever seen and controlled it with the strange medicine object Rabbit had seen hanging in his grandfather's lodge. It was a shiny device, designed to be placed in a horse's mouth. A ring encircled the lower jaw, and bits of tinkling material that sparkled like the sides of the minnows in the still pools of the creek hung from its corners. This elk-dog medicine of Heads Off was one of the most revered objects of the People and was used only ceremonially now.

Rabbit had wondered sometimes whether his own interest and delight in working with elk-dogs was associated with the fur on his face. It was said that the faraway hair-faced tribe of his grandfather was skilled with elk-dogs.

He called out and waited for his grandmother to lift the door flap. She smiled and beckoned him inside.

Tall One, the graceful old lady was called. She was nearly as tall as Rabbit, with flashing dark eyes and a quick smile. It was from this branch of the family that he had inherited his lanky frame and his taller-than-usual height.

The youth stooped to enter, straightened in the dim lodge, and nodded to the seated figure across the fire.

"*Ah-koh*, Grandfather, Grandmother."

He paused, uncertain as to how to proceed. Tall One spoke.

"Yes, my son, you seek your vision?"

Heads Off, after most of a lifetime of living with this woman, still marveled at her quick mind and powers of observation.

Of course, he now realized, it could be no other mission. A young man of fifteen, no, it was sixteen winters, carrying weapons and a waterskin but not supplies. It required little reasoning to see that young Rabbit was prepared for a journey during which he would eat nothing. Such a fast would, of course, be carried out during his vision quest.

Heads Off could hardly believe that this, his youngest grandchild, was old enough to seek his vision. In a way, he envied the young man. Heads Off had never had a vision quest. He had come to the People as Juan Garcia, a young Spanish officer, injured and lost, separated from his unit on the prairies of New Spain.

At first, he had been prevented from leaving by circumstance. A broken lance, a pregnant mare, the onset of winter. By the time his departure had become a possibility, it no longer seemed important. He had become Heads Off, a warrior of the People, his fortunes one with theirs.

His name, even, was one bestowed by the People. At their first contact, the scouts had seen him take off his officer's helmet, and for a moment it appeared that he was removing his head. *Aiee*, that part of his life seemed of another world now.

He turned his attention again to his grandson, rising to embrace him.

"May your path be smooth, my son."

The couple stood outside the lodge to watch young Rabbit pick his way across the stream and start up the opposite hill. Near its crest, he turned to wave and then was gone.

Rabbit traveled rapidly. His chosen place was a long day's travel, but he hoped to reach it before darkness. The long sunny days of the Moon of Thunder allowed more time for travel. He stopped to rest with Sun Boy directly overhead and chewed a strip of dried meat. His actual fast would not begin until he reached his destination. He rose, drank deeply from a cold spring among the rocks, and impatiently moved ahead.

Even so, Sun Boy had painted himself red and extinguished his torch to go to his lodge on the Other Side before Rabbit stood on the promontory he had selected. There was only a faint orange afterglow in the west.

Methodically, he began his preparations. From this time on, everything would move in a careful ritual.

He had brought an armful of dry fuel from the wooded valley below. He arranged the sticks to be readily available, and by light of the rising full moon, he made two more trips down the hill to obtain wood.

It was now necessary to build a fire. Rabbit cut a stick the thickness of his thumb from a dogwood growth below the hill's rim and fashioned a short fire bow with a thong from his pouch. He drew forth his fire-making materials, gathered dry tinder, and began to twirl the spindle in the socket of the other fire stick. In the space of a few heartbeats, white smoke arose, and soon a glowing coal could be seen near the spindle's tip. Skillfully, he lifted the glowing speck on a tiny nest of shredded cedar bark and began to blow softly to breathe life into the fire.

There was a sudden burst of bright yellow flame, and Rabbit thrust the blazing tinder under his carefully laid kindling. The growing light from the fire began to push the shadows back, enlarging the circle that was now Rabbit's home for the coming days. Solemnly, he stood, arms upraised, to chant the ancient Song for Fire of the People.

He spread his robe and placed his waterskin near at hand. From his pouch he took the last stick of dried meat, breaking it precisely in half. He gave half to the fire, to ask the goodwill of the spirits of this place, and chewed the other. It would be his last food for the duration of his fast, at least three suns.

Rabbit took a sip from the waterskin and settled back on his robe. There was no question of sleep. He was far too excited, too ready for the events to come in the next few days. He watched the slow turn of the stars and the shadows the moon cast across the distant prairie. Life was good.

3

>> >> >>

It seemed he had blinked his eyes for only a moment, but it was daylight. *Aiee*, he had slept after aL! Rabbit rose, fed a few sticks to rejuvenate his fire, and laced the east to greet the rising of Sun Boy with the Morning Song.

He had always enjoyed the quiet of early morning, watching the prairie awaken. A deer and her fawn moved cautiously across the meadow below to drink at the stream. Their presence alarmed a great blue heron, which rose majestically above the trees and departed to seek hunting places with less disturbance.

In the distance, small bands of antelope, elk, and buffalo grazed quietly or ambled toward watering places. A coyote and her halfgrown pups angled across a brushy slope in search of game. The young man smiled. The pups were receiving a lesson in hunting, exactly as the young of the People were instructed in the Rabbit Society.

He took a few sips of water and lay propped on an elbow on his robe. Rabbit hated to admit it, but he was bored. His anticipation of the thrill of a vision quest had produced a massive letdown when the time actually came.

9

He was moderately hungry but consoled himself with the knowledge that it would pass. The pangs would give way to an exhilarating clearness of thought, he knew. The fast required patience.

It was not until the following day that Rabbit began to experience a quickness of mind. He felt that he could see farther, hear better, and run faster than ever before. Even his sense of smell seemed more acute. At last he was experiencing the exhilaration he sought.

He doubted that he would be able to sleep that night to receive his vision but had no trouble drifting off. The dreams were unlike those of normal sleep. There was more clarity, more color, and, above all, more insight. In his vision, Rabbit walked across the prairie, stimulated by an understanding of all things, which he had never before experienced. He actually felt the fear in the heart of a crouching meadow mouse under a tuft of grass and the relentless purpose of the silent snake that stalked it.

He exulted in the strength and majesty of a great bull elk that stood on a hillock to survey his band of cows and felt the quiet contentment of a herd of grazing buffalo.

An eagle swept past him, on fixed wings, and Rabbit found that, by concentrating, his spirit could soar with the unfettered freedom of the great bird.

Yet, through all, the young man had a curious detachment. It was as if he were aware that these things were part of a dreamworld, even as he experienced them. The feeling was strong that there was more to come. He wakened, looked around him at the moonlit prairie, and took a sip from his waterskin. He could hardly wait to return to the dreamworld.

His next vision seemed to begin where the previous one was interrupted. He was soaring like the eagle over vast areas of the plains. There seemed to be a purposeful direction, though he did not understand why. He had the feeling that the distance involved would represent many sleeps for a traveler on foot.

The land in his vision changed. Below him, the grass was shorter and more sparse. There were broken hills with stone outcroppings in unfamiliar shades of color. In the distance, a blue line that must indicate mountains could be seen. Rabbit had never seen mountains but recognized the unmistakable appearance.

Then, without recognizing exactly how he had arrived there, he was among people. It was a village much like his own, with children and dogs running at play and women dressing skins to tan for robes.

Yet, over all, there was an unmistakable feeling of trouble. In his dream, Rabbit walked among these people, unseen, as they moved about their daily tasks, and the mood was one of fear and dread. It was an uncomfortable vision, the feeling so powerful that Rabbit wakened, peering anxiously into the dark shadows of the night. He grasped his short bow and assumed a defensive stance, arrow fitted and ready. But there was nothing. It was some time before he was able to settle back, listening to the comforting familiarity of the night sounds.

At last he slept again, and the vision was completely different. He stood on a windswept plain, alone. He carried a rawhide rope, and his purpose seemed to be to catch one of the horses which dotted the landscape. Rabbit smiled, relaxed and confident now. Here was something he understood.

He moved among the grazing animals, in harmony with their spirits. A mare raised her head to look curiously at him, but her attitude and the reflection of her thoughts showed no alarm.

Rabbit moved softly among them, still feeling their feelings as if he were inside their heads. He seemed to understand their thoughts better than his own, which were blurred and becoming confused. He seemed to be searching for a specific animal, but the one he sought was not among the numerous elk-dogs scattered across the dream landscape. He had no clear idea why he sought this horse. Would he even recognize it when he found it?

Rabbit made his way, still searching, toward the ridge of a low hill to his left. He had partially ascended the slope when he sensed a change in the attitude of the scattered herd.

It did not have the feeling of fear but of excitement, an unusual, thrilling stimulation. It was like the trembling anticipation at the beginning of the hunt, when the scouts have signaled the nearness of the buffalo but the sign to move forward has not yet been given. Rabbit could tell that each of the scattered horses felt the same emotion. The situation was tense, expectant.

From the corner of his eye, he saw a crow sweeping out of the misty distance of the dream. The bird flew nearer, perched on a scrubby bush almost within arm's reach, and cocked its head quizzically to one side. Looking him directly in the eye, it emitted three loud cries and flew away.

Rabbit watched the creature fly out of sight, puzzled. Since he had entered the strange dreamworld of his vision quest, he had been able to understand, to be inside the thoughts, the fears of all the creatures he encountered. It had not been so with the crow. It had seemed that the bird had attempted to tell him something, to attract his attention. Somehow, the young man felt that he was failing to understand. The dream became uneasy, confusing, and he glanced around anxiously.

A movement at the top of the slope caught his eye, and Rabbit turned. There, just rising from the other side to stand on the crest, was the most magnificent stallion he had ever seen. The proud head and arching neck gave the look of a chief, a leader of elk-dogs. Wide-set, clear-seeing eyes gazed across the prairie with confidence. The broad chest and long, supple muscles told of great strength and speed. The stallion appeared to be a young animal, glorying in the first fullness of his maturity.

The most remarkable feature, however, was the animal's color. From nose to tail, the young stallion practically shone with a glow like the red embers of a dying fire. Highlights along the neck, the massive hip, and the shoulder reflected the sunlight in sparkling iridescence.

"*Aiee!*" breathed Rabbit, awed by the spectacle. "There was never such a horse!"

He closed his eyes for a moment against the brilliance of reflected light from the glossy coat. It seemed that he could still see the animal through closed lids, the bright curls of flame darting from the flowing mane and tail.

Then, he was wakening, and the light in his eyes was that from the fire of Sun Boy's torch as it thrust above earth's rim. Shaken and unsure, Rabbit rolled over and sat up. He looked quickly around, half expecting to see the horse, but there was no living creature near him. Yet, it had been so real!

In the distance, as daylight strengthened, he could see again scattered elk and buffalo but no horses. What did it mean, this vision of his? Could the horse be his spirit-guide?

Rabbit tossed a handful of sticks on the embers of his fire and rose to greet the day with the Morning Song. As he finished and sat back down to take a sip from his waterskin, he noticed a crow perched on a nearby dogwood.

"*Ah-koh*, my brother," the young man greeted in whimsical amusement, remembering the bird in his dream. "Are you my medicine guide?"

The bird stood for a moment, then settled its feet on the branch and shook out the dampness of the dew from shining black wings. It cocked a quizzical eye at the young man, and he somehow felt that the bright eye looked into his very soul.

Then the crow bobbed its tail and raised its head to utter three raucous cries, exactly as in his dream. Before the astonished Rabbit could react, the bird spread its wings and rose effortlessly to beat its way slowly across the valley to the northwest.

Rabbit sprang to his feet, tempted to cry out and run after the disappearing creature.

Aiee, how stupid, he thought. To see one's medicine animal and fail to even recognize it!

4

>> >> >>

Rabbit waited impatiently for sleep to come again, for more visions to complete his understanding. Through the long hours of daylight he sat or lay with eyes closed, but to no avail. It was not until darkness had fallen that exhaustion overcame him and sleep covered him like a gently spread robe.

But there was no vision. The sleep was pure, dreamless and refreshing, and seemed to the sleeper to last only a moment. When he wakened in the gray-pink mists of the next day's dawn, he was disappointed. Surely, there would be more to the vision quest. There were too many unanswered questions.

The day wore on, like any other day, while Rabbit grew more and more frustrated. The thing which finally convinced him was the return of Rain Maker, marching again from the west. Wrapped in fluffy robes of white turning to dirty gray as it advanced, the storm towered over the distant prairie. By the time he could hear the far-off boom of Rain Maker's drum, Rabbit was gathering his few belongings and preparing to travel.

Even as he did so, he felt a certain sense of guilt.

Somehow, he should have been able to gain more meaning, more understanding from his visions. He wondered if other vision seekers emerged with this confusion in their thoughts. It would be difficult to know. One's vision quest was a thing so personal, so private that it was not usually discussed. Most of the People did not even speak of their medicine animal. To ask another person questions about the experience would be unthinkable.

Rabbit hurried down the bluff and entered the dense growth of giant trees at its base before the first fat drops of rain began to fall. He built a fire against the damp chill and squatted over it with his robe across his head and shoulders. Here he would wait until Rain Maker passed.

Shortly before dark, the young man chanced to see the outline of a squirrel through the falling drizzle. The creature was sitting on the horizontal limb of a great oak tree a few steps away, hunched in the rain and partially sheltered against the massive trunk. The animal's tail was drawn up over its back, the long hairs fluffed erect to provide additional shelter.

Here was food, and Rabbit was beginning to be eager to break his fast. At the thought, his stomach squirmed noisily. The amusing idea struck him that the sound might frighten the squirrel away, but it seemed not to notice. The animal sat frozen, apparently considering itself invisible.

Rabbit slowly shed his robe and fitted an arrow to his bowstring. He hesitated a moment, hating to risk a valuable arrow on this sort of a shot. A miss would send the arrow into the thick tangle of brush and timber to be almost surely lost. What a waste, to expend an arrow that could fell a buffalo on the chance of obtaining a meager meal such as this.

These thoughts lasted only a moment. Life was full of small risks and must be lived aggressively. In this case, it merely meant that he must not miss. He drew the arrow to his chin, the string twanged dully, and the fat squirrel tumbled to the ground.

In a short while, the skinned and gutted carcass was broiling over his fire, melting fat dripping to hiss against the coals. He turned the dogwood stick occasionally, the smells of cooking reminding him how ravenously hungry he was.

The squirrel was tough and stringy, dry by comparison with the rich fat of buffalo hump ribs. But this was not a fair comparison, Rabbit realized as he nibbled the last fragments of meat from the red-purple bones. The squirrel represented only a temporary emergency or novelty ration for the People, while the buffalo was the staple food on which their entire culture depended.

When Rabbit arrived back at the camp of the People the following evening, he could hardly wait to talk with his father. Yet, he hardly knew what to talk about. How could he describe the strange feeling, the intense emotional attraction for the horse in his vision? More important, *why* had it been so?

He had no clear idea what he had expected, but it was certainly nothing like this. There was an urge, a driving desire, which he did not understand. It pulled at him to go, to move, to do something.

But what? The urge was misty, unformed, like that which he sometimes felt when he stood and watched the long lines of geese in the Moon of Falling Leaves. Rabbit would listen to their traveling song until they were out of sight and heading on their southward journey, and he would be thrilled anew each time. There was a strange urge to join the great birds on their journey, and he would look wistfully after them, silently calling into the sky.

"Wait for me!"

It was this sort of longing that the memory of the Dream-horse stirred within him. Rabbit did not understand the vague call to do something not clearly defined.

The opportunity to speak with his father did not come until after twilight had fallen. His mother had cooked a great quantity of broiled hump ribs, and the young man's appetite after days of fasting was ready to do justice to the repast. For a time he thought his overfull stomach would reject such outrageous abuse, but gradually he began to feel better.

Rabbit and his parents were reclining before the lodge in the cool evening. Fragrant smoke from Owl's pipe curled lazily upward to be lost in the deepening night sky. There were the calm sounds of the camp, a child's tired complaint, the soft snuffle of a tethered buffalo horse behind a nearby lodge. Night insects chirped to the accompaniment of the stream's murmuring song. Finally, Rabbit approached the subject uppermost in his mind.

"Father," he began hesitantly, "I have seen strange things in my visions."

Owl said nothing but puffed quietly on his stone pipe. His son would continue when he was ready.

"There was a horse, a horse of powerful medicine." Rabbit paused, unsure.

After a long moment, Owl spoke.

"Yes, my son? This was your medicine animal?"

"I think not, Father. It was a different feeling."

He had decided not to mention the crow. One's medicine guide was a very private thing. Some people lived their entire lives without revealing the source of their medicine. Maybe the time would come when he would discuss this part of his dream with his father, but for now he would keep it to himself.

The medicine man was again waiting in silence. The story would come in due time

"It was in a faraway place," Rabbit continued dreamily, "under the shadow of mountains."

Now the tale tumbled forth more rapidly. A torrent of words poured out like the rise of a prairie stream in response to a sudden rain upstream.

"What does it mean, Father?" Rabbit finished with a question.

The hairs on the back of his neck bristled with the excitement of reliving the dream, and his palms were wet with tension.

Owl thought a moment, taking three long puffs on his pipe.

"I am not certain, my son. There was no instruction, no feel of what you must do, what is to be?"

Rabbit shook his head. He attempted to explain his feelings about the urge to follow the geese, but he felt that he did so rather ineffectively. Still, his father seemed to understand.

"Yes," Owl nodded, "there is a need to do something. We must find what it is."

He drew a long sigh.

"My husband," Willow spoke for the first time, "it is a

matter of elk-dogs. Would not Heads Off know much of elk-dog medicine?"

Of course! Owl became almost excited. His own medicine was primarily that of the buffalo, but his father had more powerful elk-dog medicine than anyone in the tribe. *Aiee*, of course! Heads Off had brought the First Elk-dog to the People. Who would know better than he of elk-dog matters?

Quickly, the two men rose and walked through the camp to the lodge of the chief. Owl rapped on the taut lodge skin and called out.

"Mother? Father? It is Owl and your grandson, Rabbit!"

They were welcomed inside, though it was apparent that Heads Off and Tall One were in the process of retiring. This was obviously an urgent visit.

"*Aiee*, Rabbit!" his grandmother spoke. "You are back from your quest. It was good?"

"That is why we are here, Grandmother. I would ask of elk-dog medicine."

Heads Off motioned them to sit, and the men lighted pipes. Any discussion would flow better amid the sweet incense of fragrant smoke.

Rabbit poured forth his story, more smoothly this time. The chief listened intently but at the end shook his head in frustration.

"I do not know, Rabbit."

He turned to Owl and spread his hands in frustration.

"I know little of vision quests, my son. I have never had one."

Rabbit was startled. He had never realized that fact, but of course it was reasonable. Heads Off had been a grown man, a proven warrior, before he came to the People.

"But Grandfather," Rabbit protested, "you know of elk-dogs!"

"Rabbit feels that he must search for this spirit-horse," explained Owl.

Again, Rabbit was startled. He had not been able to quite accept this as the dream's meaning. Now that it had been shaped into words by his father, however, the meaning began to take form. Stranger things had been.

Almost in the space of a few heartbeats, a sense of

direction was descending over the young man. He would attempt a journey, a quest to search for the Dream-horse.

His grandfather was speaking.

"If you are to search for this chief of elk-dogs, my son," he advised, "you will need powerful elk-dog medicine."

Heads Off rose and reverently took down a shiny object from its place of honor above his sleeping robes. With deliberate ceremony, he placed its thong around the neck of the young man. The beautifully crafted steel and silver Spanish bit bumped gently against the front of Rabbit's shirt, firelight reflecting from silver dangles.

Rabbit was overwhelmed. It was the most important event of his life. His wildest fantasies had never suggested this possibility. That he should be entrusted with the elk-dog medicine, the most revered of the People, was beyond belief.

Already, he could feel its power penetrating and warming his body, bringing strength and purpose.

5

» » »

Rabbit sighted between the ears of his horse at a hilltop on the horizon and nudged the animal into a distance-eating trot. He had stopped to allow time to graze and to rest his own travel-weary bones.

Fourteen sleeps, now, he had traveled, with no particular goal except that he must move in a northwesterly direction. His vision had indicated it. Why, he did not yet know. True to his easygoing nature, Rabbit assumed that when the proper time came he would find out.

He knew that he had traveled well. His horse was good. The young man had been pleased and flattered by the gift. He was preparing to depart when his cousin Running Eagle and her husband had approached.

This was one of the most prominent couples in the tribe, owners of many horses. The fame of Running Eagle, the warrior woman, and her constant companion, Long Walker, had been known across the plains. Young Rabbit had been proud to claim family ties. Now married, and with a child of their own, the couple led a quieter life.

But now they approached the lodge of Rabbit's parents. Running Eagle was leading a gray horse.

"*Ah-koh* Uncle, and to you, Willow," she greeted Rabbit's father and nodded to his mother.

Then she turned to the young man.

"Rabbit," she smiled, "you go on a long quest. You must be well mounted."

She handed him the rope that was attached to the jaw of the gray horse.

"Her name is Gray Cloud. She is the daughter of my own mare, Gray Cat, who carries the blood of horse chiefs. Hers is the family of the First Elk-dog, brought by our grandfather, Heads Off."

Rabbit had heard the story many times, so many that as a child he had become bored and tired of it. Yet this time, he was impressed as never before. What an honor that his cousin and her husband would give him one of the finest of their horses for his quest. With such a mount and elk-dog medicine to guide him, how could he fail in his mission?

And with the help of his medicine bird, of course. He kept forgetting the strange, puzzling appearance of the crow in all this, whatever it might mean. He had seen many crows as he rode, but none that appeared to be *the* crow of his vision.

The horse proved to be excellent. Rabbit felt that he had never ridden an animal of such quality before. Distance slid behind them as smoothly as day follows night. Rabbit had counted on his fingers the fourteen sleeps since he left the People and verified his count by the moon. It had been full when he departed and was only a narrow slice in the dying rays of Sun Boy's torch last evening.

There had been one narrow escape. Seven suns ago, he had nearly blundered into a hunting party of Head Splitters. Actually, it had been sheer good fortune that he had seen the other riders before they saw him.

Rabbit had stopped to water the gray mare and dismounted in the white gravel of the creek bed. While the mare drank, he stepped a few paces to a small rise to study the prairie ahead. As he reached the crest of the hillock, he was completely surprised to see a line of mounted warriors filing over the next ridge. They moved down the wandering game trail like a column of ants, one behind the other.

Quickly, Rabbit dropped to a concealed position and peered out between sumac stems. He did not think he had been seen.

The riders were only a few hundred paces away, and in the space of a breath or two he realized the worst. This was a well-armed party, some fifteen strong. They were probably on a routine hunt, but it could quickly become a hunt with himself as the quarry.

Almost instantly, he realized his greatest danger. His mare, sensing the approach of others of her kind, might call out to them and reveal his position. Frantically, he slid backward down the slope. If he could only reach the horse before she scented or heard the approaching animals.

As quietly as he could, he stepped across the shifting clatter of the rocky beach and reached for the nose of the mare. With his hand firmly muzzling her against any outcry, Rabbit glanced quickly around for a place of concealment. He had already discarded the possibility of attempting to run. He would be seen immediately. Although his mare might outdistance the enemy at first, it was too risky. Any slipup, a stumble, would be the end. In addition, pursuit by a large number of riders would allow them to press the fugitive constantly. They could pace themselves, allowing one or two to press while others saved their horses to press in turn. The gray mare would be under constant, unrelenting pressure to best one pursuer after another. She might be able to accomplish this, but Rabbit was willing to attempt it as a last resort only. He would attempt to hide and could still run if discovered.

An island in the shallow, sandy stream presented a possibility. The low strip of land was thickly covered by a growth of plum bushes. He was already leading the horse toward the shelter of the dense foliage.

It was difficult to wade, lead the animal, and hold her nose to prevent her crying out, all at the same time. There was no time to spare. He could already hear the voices of the enemy hunters and the muffled rhythm of their horses' hooves. He plunged into the thicket, his hands and face scratched and bleeding from the thorny plum branches.

The foliage had hardly fallen into place behind Rabbit and the mare when the first of the riders came into sight. The man called back to his followers, pointing to the stream. They clattered carelessly down the slope and began to allow thirsty horses to drink. Men dismounted and splashed in the knee-deep current, laughing and joking.

Rabbit carefully tied a thong around his mare's nose to muzzle her voice. It was too risky to hold her with his hand alone. A toss of her head and she could cry out to her counterparts, only a short bow shot away. The animal's slender ears pricked forward, striving to hear better the sounds of watering horses and men.

The next few moments would be the critical ones. Hopefully, the enemy party would not explore the area thoroughly. Rabbit knew that his tracks were plain to see in the soft earth of the stream's bank.

He peered through the plum thicket and watched in fascination while the Head Splitters relaxed. Those who had dismounted moved slightly upstream from their horses to find cleaner water to drink. This brought them closer to his hiding place, now hardly more than a stone's throw.

Suddenly a warrior called out an urgent warning and pointed to the water in which they stood. The laughter and casual conversation stopped as the entire party paused to look.

Rabbit realized the cause for their sudden reaction. He could easily see, in the sparkling clear current of the stream, the cloudy stretch of muddied water, stirred by his own feet and those of the gray mare.

The excited murmur of the enemy party continued. Men reached for weapons, some remounted. One warrior spoke loudly and pointed directly at the plum thicket on the little island.

Now, Rabbit conceded, the time had come to test the mettle of the gray mare. He prepared to swing up. The enemy pressed forward, spreading across the width of the streambed as they advanced. The nervous mare, sensing a race, stamped a front foot impatiently.

Almost simultaneously she snorted, the muffled snort that a horse may still make when muzzled. There was an answering snort from the thick brush a few steps away.

A large animal rose to its feet and crashed through the thicket into the stream.

The buffalo clattered across the narrow strip of water and lumbered up the slope, pursued by a handful of horsemen. The rest of the group laughed and relaxed, turning again to the stream.

Rabbit was so startled that he nearly cried out aloud. He had been completely unaware of the presence of the bull. It was apparently an aged loner, an outcast from the herds. It had sought shelter from the heat of the day and the biting of insects among the plum bushes. Apparently the Head Splitters were willing to explain the muddied waters of the stream by the bull's presence. For this, Rabbit was grateful.

The hunting party now prepared to camp for the night in the grassy flat next to the stream. Hunters returned, having downed the buffalo just beyond the rise. The meat from an aged bull would be stringy and tough but better than none. They started fires and began to cook.

Rabbit lay low in the thicket. Evening was near, and the night would be dark after the setting of the narrow moon. He relaxed as much as possible in the cramped and thorny thicket, giving the restless mare a reassuring pat occasionally.

By full darkness the Head Splitters were well fed, relaxed, and unobservant. Carefully, he led the mare upstream a short way. Their noises were indistinguishable from those of the enemy's own horses as they grazed and watered along the creek.

Safely out of the reach of the firelight, the youth swung to the mare's back and removed the constricting thong from her nose. She snorted and blew through her nostrils in relief as they left the stream and struck a ground-eating lope.

Rabbit glanced to his right at the Real-star, hanging fixed in the northern sky, to establish his northwesterly direction. By the time the Head Splitters awakened he would be far away.

6

»» »» »»

Rabbit knew that he had traveled far by the changing country. Gradually, he had left behind the tall grasses of his native hills. They had given way to short, dusty blue-green buffalo grass. Curly and thick, this nutritious plant was prized as horse pasture by the People, but in specific areas only. Here it appeared to be the major plant of the region. The mare Gray Cloud was staying in excellent condition on such forage.

But during the last few days Rabbit had noticed large areas where even the buffalo grass was thin and sparse. The earth was dry, and the watercourses were sandy. He became alarmed one evening when a fringe of willows along a winding gully failed to mark the expected water.

Rabbit was kneeling to feel the damp sand in the streambed when he was startled by a sudden snort. A buck deer seemed to materialize from nowhere and clattered up out of the gully and away.

The gray mare raised her ears and started eagerly toward the spot so recently vacated by the deer. The youth rose and followed.

In a low spot in the sandy creek bed, deer or other

animals had pawed a depression perhaps an arm's length across. Water was seeping into the hole from below. He dropped to his knees and began to dig like a dog after a ground squirrel.

As the depression deepened, water came more rapidly until both man and horse were able to quench their thirst. Rabbit camped for the night and drank all he could hold in addition to filling his waterskin before departure next morning.

Now, Rabbit was beginning to feel uneasy for the first time about his entire quest. He was moving into ever more inhospitable country. It was not unlike the barren desert of his dream. There had been no further directive from his medicine crow.

He did not know how far in this direction he could travel. The People had never come this far. Even the Mountain band of the People kept to the south of this area.

Worst of all was that he did not know what to fear. He believed that he was well out of the country of the Head Splitters, but he had no way of knowing which tribes were active here. In his own country, a traveler could often inquire of the Growers, who traded with all. But it had been many days since he left the last village of Growers.

Of course, he mused. How can there be Growers where nothing grows?

He had not expected to miss the Growers, strange people with permanent lodges dug partway into the ground. True, he had spent a couple of nights in Grower villages for security. Even an enemy would not attack him while a guest in another tribe's village. He had slept outside. The People had a deep-seated distrust of permanent lodges. Besides, there was the vague fear that lice and other parasites inhabit the dwellings of Growers.

Now, Rabbit would have welcomed the chance to talk to almost anyone. He found himself talking aloud to his horse more frequently, simply for the sound of a human voice.

In addition, Growers could have informed him of which tribes, if any, were active in the area, how aggressive and dangerous they might be. But there were no Growers.

That evening Rabbit camped in another of the dry

washes that seemed to be typical to this forbidding country. He dug a hole for water in the manner now becoming familiar and then sat chewing some of the last of his
dry pemmican. Before another day passed, he would be
forced to stop and hunt for meat.

If there was any to be found, he thought glumly. Game
had been increasingly scarce as the grass had thinned.
Never had his quest seemed so hopeless, so undirected,
so far away.

He built a fire, using dead twigs from the greasy brush
that grew along the creek bed. The warmth was not
needed for the body, but one must also warm the spirit.
He gazed morosely into the glowing coals as Sun Boy
retired to the west and the stars began to appear.

A snort from his mare warned him, and he started to
rise, then altered his move to reach for a handful of
sticks for the fire. Rabbit felt the presence of an observer
as he tried to move casually The hair prickled on the
back of his neck, and he expected an overt attack of
some sort at any moment. How would it come? As an
arrow, searching from the darkness? He fought back the
temptation to run.

Still pretending to be unaware, he frantically searched
the opposite slope with his eyes. The mare stood, ears
pricked forward, staring into the night. The newly added
fuel began to blaze, and its light crowded the shadows
together and pushed them back against the blackness of
the dark slope.

Suddenly a figure appeared, only a few paces away,
across the sandy wash. Rabbit had not seen the man
move. The newcomer seemed to have been there all the
time. Now, as Rabbit stared, two more men emerged to
stand beside the tall, heavyset one, who was apparently
the leader. Momentarily, Rabbit wondered how many
more warriors were hidden by the darkness, perhaps even
behind him. Again, his skin crawled uncomfortably.

The strangers were of no tribe Rabbit had seen before.
The garments they wore were cut in a different manner,
and there was a vague unfamiliarity in their weapons,
their manner of braiding their hair, and their strange
blue-white facial paint.

The paint itself was alarming. Ordinarily, men would

not paint themselves unless they were engaged in a hunt
or a war party. He hesitated to pursue that thought further.

Rabbit wondered if these warriors used the sign language. He held up a hand in greeting and began to use the
signs.

"Greetings. How are you called?" There was a long
pause, and Rabbit began to think there was no understanding. Finally, the man who appeared to be the leader
stepped forward into the circle of firelight.

"We are called Blue Paint People. Who are you?"

Rabbit took a long breath and thought rapidly. The
outcome of this encounter was certainly in question. He
might be killed. Regardless, he wished to present as dignified an appearance as possible. He simply could not tell
these capable-looking warriors that his name was Rabbit.
It was a childish name.

He cleared his throat and tried to speak in a mature and
confident manner, accompanying his speech with sign
talk.

"I am called Horse Seeker. I am of a tribe called Elk-
dog People." Rabbit gestured vaguely in the direction he
had come.

Cautiously, he rose, taking care to show that he held
no weapon in either hand. The strangers approached him
carefully.

"You are alone?" the leader gestured.

Rabbit hesitated, hating to answer the truth. The hesitation itself was an answer. The big man nodded and
motioned to his companions, who began to rummage
through Rabbit's supplies. They seemed disappointed at
their meager loot. Two others joined the group at the
fire, speaking in their own tongue. One led the mare
Gray Cloud by a rope around her jaw.

The chief looked the mare over appreciatively, nodded,
and turned back to Rabbit.

"You are alone."

It was a statement, not a question.

"Is this your horse?"

Rabbit was irritated.

"You have said there is no one else here! Whose could
it be?"

The situation was beginning to look desperate.

"Where are your people?" The chief was insisting.

Rabbit shrugged, hoping to keep them guessing.

"Nearby."

"That is not true."

The firelight reflected a gleam of silver from the Spanish bit on Rabbit's chest. The stranger stepped forward to look more closely.

"What is this?"

"It is my medicine. It is very dangerous to those who do not understand it."

He had hoped to dissuade the strangers from interest in the object, but the chief laughed aloud. He was obviously more impressed by its power and beauty than by any potential danger. He drew a short belt knife and quickly severed the thong that held the silver-mounted bit.

Rabbit's first impulse was to attack the man, to fight to the death in defense of this important amulet of the People. Good judgment restrained him. If he were killed, there would be no one to retrieve the all-important medicine object. No one would even know where to look. Even so, he must protest.

"It is an evil thing you do." he warned.

"The evil falls on you," the other laughed.

The warriors were finished plundering his camp, and their chief turned away. Rabbit was so certain that they intended to kill him that he was half prepared when the terse command came. The big man half turned after he had taken a step or two and muttered a single guttural command.

Rabbit, though he understood not a word of the strangers' tongue, was certain of the meaning. If the big warrior had spoken the command in the language of the People, it could have been no clearer.

"Kill him!"

Rabbit started to turn at a sound behind him. From the corner of his eye he glimpsed a descending weapon. He tried to dodge, but too late.

The war club struck a glancing blow above his ear, and his senses exploded like the crash of real-fire in the Moon of Thunder. Then there was blackness.

7

>> >> >>

Rabbit woke slowly, his confused brain refusing to function at once. At first, he considered that he must be dead. It would be the expected thing, after a blow such as he had received. In a few heartbeats, however, his senses began to tell him otherwise.

Painfully, he sorted out the sensations. Most prominent was the throbbing in his head, pounding with a rhythmic thump like that of a huge dance drum. Even in his semiconscious state, instinct told him that any attempt to move would increase the painful booming inside his skull.

Among other sensations was the warmth of the sun on his cheek. It was strange, his confused thoughts told him, that he could feel the rays of Sun Boy's torch while it was yet dark. Was he dead after all? Was this the Other Side, the Spirit World? But no, one who has crossed over does not feel pain. He must be still alive.

Then why the darkness? In a moment he realized that his eyes were still closed. Something was preventing the lids from parting. Carefully, he moved his right hand to his face, rubbing at his eyes in bewilderment. His fingers encountered a rough, sticky crust of some foreign material which effectively caked his right eyelid closed. Moving his head was a major effort, but he managed to roll slightly from his face-downward position in the sand to feel for his left eye. It was with a great sense of relief that he was able to rub the left lid open and discover that he could partially see.

Reasoning was returning. He now realized that blood from the massive head wound above his ear had trickled down into his right eye and puddled in the sand beneath his face.

He attempted to focus his partial vision and identified another sound that had puzzled him. The dull buzz was produced by a myriad of lazy green flies which gathered at the sticky puddle in the sand.

Rabbit's hand sought the wound on his head, and he winced as his probing fingers encountered a tender lump, half the size of his fist. His right eye was still stuck shut with dried and clotted blood. He must have water to loosen the crusted mass.

At the thought of water, he was ravenously thirsty. There, directly before him and hardly two paces away, was the drinking pool he had scooped out the night before. It might as well have been a day's travel away, it seemed to Rabbit. The very thought of moving at all seemed beyond all possibility.

Mustering all his strength he raised to his elbows and drew himself forward a little. The exertion made the pounding worse in his head, and he lay still a long while. Little by little, with frequent rest, he crawled toward the pool.

When he could at last thrust his mouth into the tepid water, he drank long and rested for a time. Then he submerged his entire face, rubbing at the caked blood in his eye. It was a relief to see again.

He felt better now, but he still did not feel like moving. The water in his stomach made him a little queasy, and he hesitated to try to sit up. Finally, exhausted, he slept.

This time he was awakened by the harsh cawing of a crow. The noise grated on sensitive ears and made his head throb painfully again. Nevertheless, he managed to open his eyes and rise to one elbow. There, almost within arm's reach, stood a large black bird with a wrinkled head.

Rabbit had never seen a buzzard at so close a distance before. The hooked beak looked wickedly sharp and efficient. Little shiny eyes peered from the naked red skin of the bird's face. The carrion eater had been attracted by the motionless figure. Even now, circling shadows told of others of its kind dropping in slow spirals to join the feast.

It was fortunate, Rabbit reflected, that he had awakened. A single slashing stroke from the wickedly hooked beak could have destroyed an eye or left an ear or part of his face mutilated for life. What had awakened him in time? The crow, he remembered now, and looked around.

Flying away at a little distance was a lone crow. As it moved rapidly out of the stream's bed and over the plain, it uttered a series of long-drawn cries. Rabbit was certain that the bird turned and looked at him just before it moved over the rim of the gully and out of sight.

Aiee! He was always failing to recognize his medicine animal, his spirit-guide. At least the crow had wakened him in time. Frustrated, he turned back to the buzzard.

The bird thrust a quizzical stare at him and took a step closer. Rabbit could smell the creature, still reeking with the aroma of its last meal of rotted carrion. He waved a hand at the bird, startling it into a jump backward.

"No, my friend," he spoke to the buzzard, "I am not ready to be your next meal."

As if in understanding, the bird spread its ponderous wings and sprang into the air. Clumsy, beating wing strokes pulled it upward until it found a rising air current.

Then the bird became a thing of grace and beauty, circling upward to join others far above.

Now, for the first time, Rabbit was able to think clearly enough to evaluate the seriousness of his situation. Slowly the facts sank home.

He had failed. Failed miserably and completely, in every way. His quest, the mission that had caused him to leave the Tallgrass Hills of the People, seemed far away and insignificant. He had betrayed the confidence that his family had in him.

The horse, Gray Cloud, among the finest of the People, was gone. His cousin might forgive him, but he could never forgive himself. He had failed to be alert and had allowed the strangers to approach before he became aware of their presence.

His worst loss, though, was the loss of the bit, the elk-dog medicine of the People. Rabbit's heart sank at the thought. The People had prospered since the day his grandfather, Heads Off, had joined them with the First Elk-dog and the powerful amulet that controlled it.

Now it was gone. Without the power of its medicine, could the People survive? The horse had become so much a part of their lives that other tribes now called them the Elk-dog People. Was this to be the end of their influence on the plains?

The thought that he might be responsible for such a tragedy to his tribe was almost more than Rabbit could bear. He sat in the dry sand and cried unashamedly.

Finally he rose to his feet, swaying like a willow in the wind, and stood trying to orient himself. He swallowed hard to keep his stomach from attempting to empty itself. Slowly, the pounding in his head decreased and settled to a steady, painful thump. His vision was still not clear, his sight fuzzy. It seemed to require more effort to focus his eyes than he had available to him.

It had still not occurred to Rabbit that his very survival was at stake. He was unfamiliar with the plants and animals of the region. His spirit was not attuned to communicate with the spirits of this strange and country.

In his mind there was only one thought. Somehow he must right his mistakes, atone for failure. He must recover the elk-dog medicine, the powerful amulet of the People.

His shimmering vision cleared somewhat, and his eyes focused on the floor of the sandy wash. There were the indentations made by Blue Paint, his companions, and their horses the previous evening.

Dully, Rabbit thought about the matter. It seemed simple enough. He had only to follow these tracks in the sand. When he overtook the enemy war party, he would recover the elk-dog amulet, retrieve his horse, and continue on his mission. If only his head would stop spinning. He choked back another wave of nausea and stepped forward, staggering.

The trail led northwest. *Aiee*, thought Rabbit, this fits

well with my mission. It is good. He could not remember much about the nature of his mission or how he came to be here. It only seemed important that his direction was northwest.

He plodded doggedly forward, driven by necessity. He must follow the enemy, recover his grandfather's medicine. Just now he could remember no more. Perhaps later, when his thoughts cleared and the throbbing in his head subsided, he could remember.

8

>> >> >>

Apparently Rabbit did have the presence of mind to pick up some of his belongings. At least when he stopped later to rest he realized he was carrying his robe. He did not recall recovering the garment from his erstwhile campsite. In fact, he remembered very little.

There were the strangers, who insolently plundered his belongings and struck him down, leaving him for dead. There were periods of time when he plodded ahead, following the vague trail in the parched sand, without remembering why he did so. He would pause, gather his thoughts through the throbbing in his head, and remember that he had a mission. Sometimes even that mission seemed vague. Its purpose had changed, somehow.

Rabbit would stop, rest a little, and force himself to think. Yes, his new mission had an urgency not required by the old one. It involved the following of the trail left by the strange chief with blue face paint and his followers. Still the young man had trouble remembering exactly why he followed the trail of the strangers. It was not for vengeance, he found himself puzzling at one time, but something similar. He must right a wrong.

Then his elusive memory would return and thought of his failure would come crashing again into his consciousness. Ultimately the despair of having lost the all-important elk-dog medicine would force him into activity again. He would rise and plod ahead.

It had seemed a great distance that he followed the tracks to where the strangers had camped for the night. Actually, it was no more than a long bow shot from his own camp. Foggily, he realized that they must have already established their camp before he arrived. How simple it had been for the others to creep upon him unsuspected in the gathering darkness. He was embarrassed at his ineptness and quickly moved on.

With the falling of night Rabbit realized that he must rest. He dug for water in the manner he had learned, drank deeply, and fell exhausted without even building a fire.

When he awoke it was to the music of coyotes, calling to each other or to the moon in their strange chuckling language. He felt better. Some things were the same anywhere. If these little brothers of the prairie looked and sounded the same here as in his own country, then the world must still be right. He found the thought comforting.

Rabbit found himself thinking more clearly now. The cool night air and the period of rest and deep sleep had cleared his head somewhat. He found motion not nearly so painful to his head, though he was still quite stiff and sore.

The gray of the eastern sky was beginning to turn to rosy pink. Rabbit waited for daylight to better assess his situation. Gradually, visibility improved to the point that he could do so.

His robe lay partially beneath him, crumpled where he had half fallen as he slumped to rest. He briefly examined himself and the immediate area for other belongings. He was almost surprised to find his short knife still at his waist. It was in its rawhide sheath, tucked beneath the fringe of his hunting shirt.

Ah, that must be it. The Blue Paints, foreign to customs of the People, might have been unaware of this traditional style of personal weapon. At any rate, they had overlooked it in their plundering.

They had apparently overlooked little else. Rabbit found virtually no other belongings except his empty waterskin on its carrying thong. This finding elated him, almost as much as the finding of the knife. He hastened to fill the skin at his water hole, to allow time for the seepage to refill so that he might drink before departure.

While he waited, Rabbit looked around for anything that might be of use to him. His fire-making equipment was gone, either stolen by the Blue Paints or overlooked in the foggy circumstances of his own departure.

It was no matter. He could make another fire set. He broke a couple of last season's dry seed stalks from a nearby yucca to carry with him for the purpose. A pebble with a dimpled depression in one side for the top of the fire spindle was added to his meager pile.

Rabbit was becoming aware of hunger. It would be necessary to obtain some sort of food as he traveled. He would be alert for opportunity, but for now there was no need. He had water and could exist for some time until food became available. More important was to follow the trail of the Blue Paints.

Sun Boy was well past the top of his daily run before Rabbit came upon the dead ashes of the Blue Paints' last night camp. He examined the site carefully, with mixed emotion.

He was dismayed that it had taken him nearly two days to cover this distance. To those he followed it had been an easy day's journey. At this rate, on foot, he would never overtake the horsemen. He must do something differently to cover more distance. If only he had a horse!

In examining the abandoned campsite, Rabbit tried to overlook nothing. He must learn all he could about these people.

The tracks indicated that he had seen most of the party. There may have been two, possibly three, left to watch their own camp and their horses while the others accosted Rabbit. Surely no more than that. There was no sign of women or children with them. It must be, then, a small war party or perhaps merely a scouting party.

A pair of worn-out moccasins lay tossed aside near a clump of brush. Rabbit examined them with interest. The pattern and the symbols of decoration were unlike any he had seen before. Their most important quality, however, was that they were worn-out.

It took a little time for the significance of this fact to penetrate Rabbit's still-foggy thought process. A man who discards moccasins must have put on a new pair. The only way in which this warrior could have had new moccasins available was to have been carrying them. Only if he were starting on a long journey would a man carry spare moccasins.

Rabbit somehow felt better. He knew much more about those he pursued now. More than they knew about him.

The big man, the chief of the party, had led a handful of his followers into territory far from home. It was a scouting thrust, an exploration of country new to the Blue Paints. Otherwise, they would have their families with them. The strangers must have been looking for game or for territory to move into and had found neither. This inhospitable area of scant water would serve neither purpose.

His next discovery was even more important. Among the ashes and partly burned sticks of the dead campfire were a few bones. Rabbit squatted and poked around curiously, wondering what animal the remains represented.

The bones appeared to be from a fairly large animal, perhaps the size of a deer. More important, they represented a recent kill. A scouting party would not carry fresh meat. Could not, in fact. Fresh meat would begin to decay immediately in the heat of Sun Boy's torch unless cut in strips for drying. A traveling party could not stop to dry meat.

So, the presence of fresh bones from last night's camp meant a fresh kill nearby, less than a day ago. Rabbit rose to scan the surrounding plain.

As he turned, the young man caught a glimpse of a large dark bird, dropping soundlessly from the sky to disappear from sight behind a low hillock. Another vulture hung aloft, circling the same area on fixed wings. Rabbit hurried in that direction.

He topped the rise to see several vultures standing near the partly stripped carcass of an antelope. A pair of coyotes crouched, snarling, challenging the birds from time to time as they came too close.

Rabbit rushed forward, waving his arms and shouting

to frighten the scavengers away. The coyotes slipped
quietly aside and out of sight, while the vultures rose
clumsily into the air, wings laboring to gain altitude.
Rabbit was beginning to think he had seen enough vultures at close distances.

He knelt and began to salvage such meat as he was
able. Already, there was the smell of decay from the offal
in the day's heat. He managed to turn the carcass and
slash a sizable chunk from the haunch that had not been
exposed to the scavengers.

It would be necessary to move on. He hoped to cover
much more distance before the fall of darkness. He rose
and glanced at the circling vultures.

"The rest is yours, my brothers," he smiled as he
turned to the trail again.

He trotted forward, thinking all the while of any way
in which he might cover more distance, to close the gap
between him and the Blue Paints. With some satisfaction, he noted that he was able to trot for periods of time
before the pounding in his head began again.

Rabbit's natural optimism began to show itself as he
trotted along the trail in the gathering twilight. He had
food, water, a mission, and a trail to follow. Things were
going exceedingly well.

9

>> >> >>

It was on the fourth day that Rabbit became anxious. His prospects for overtaking the Blue Paints seemed very poor. He had found only one more of the strangers' camp-sites, which now meant that they were two days' travel ahead of him. They seemed to be moving rapidly, scarcely pausing to hunt. At this rate, each passing day placed him two days further behind.

Rabbit pondered the problem while he stopped for a brief rest. He sat chewing a mouthful of stringy antelope meat. He had managed to dry thin strips as he traveled by threading them on willow sticks. It was a clumsy and inconvenient thing, not even to be considered under nor-mal circumstances but a necessity just now. Still, it was with great relief that he found the strips baked hard by the sun and threw away his willow twigs to make a bundle of his food supply.

Now he sat, methodically chewing, seeking a solution to his problem. Those he followed were keeping to the general course of the dry riverbed, digging the now famil-iar seep holes when necessary for water. This, Rabbit

believed, indicated a general scarcity of water in the area.
He must be cautious.

But he must also find a way to cover more distance. At
first he had wished for, even looked for, a horse. There
were none. He quickly realized that this barren country
could not attract and could not support any significant
number of grazing animals. No, he must forget the possibility of capturing a wild horse. In addition, there appeared little chance of encountering any people from
whom he might borrow, beg, or steal the needed transportation.

This thought led to another. It was well known that a
horse must spend time in foraging for food. Even in
country with rich heavy grasses, much time was spent in
feeding.

Those he followed, Rabbit now realized, were not allowing time for adequate grazing. Their horses would be
suffering, losing weight and strength, becoming weaker.
This must be, then, a forced march, a temporary situation, perhaps a return to their own country.

For some reason, he felt better. The others could not
keep this pace more than a few days, and then he could
overtake them. For the present, he would try to close the
distance between them as best he could. He would travel
by moonlight, trotting and walking alternately. Even if
he were unable to see the tracks clearly, he could continue to follow the watercourse. It gave him a sense of
satisfaction that while those he pursued were sleeping,
eating, or allowing their horses to forage a little, he
would be lessening the distance between them. He rose
and trotted on.

He stopped early that evening to sleep for a brief time
in the evening's cool. Before rolling in his robe, Rabbit
drank all the water he could hold. This would insure that
his full bladder would waken him for travel.

Near moonrise he awoke, relieved himself, and set off
at a swinging trot. This was much more pleasant traveling, he realized. Without the burning heat of Sun Boy's
torch, the night air was pleasant, cool, and comfortable.
He wished he had thought of this before. Travel at night
appeared much less tiring. Perhaps he could rest during
the day and spend more of tomorrow night in travel.

He barely paused when he came to a campsite with

ashes of several fires. It required little skill to recognize, even by moonlight, that those he followed had stopped here. He trotted on.

Once a bird startled him by rising directly from his path on soft, shadowy wings. In a heartbeat or two, he had identified it as one of the small ground-dwelling owls which he had seen in the region.

Sometime later he surprised a pair of hunting coyotes, who moved swiftly aside and then stood to stare as he passed.

Glancing back over his right shoulder, Rabbit saw the pale gray of the coming dawn begin to invade the black of the eastern sky, and he jogged on. The outlines of the rolling plain, with scrubby willows and an occasional cottonwood along the stream, became more visible in the growing light.

When the first rays of the rising sun began to warm his right shoulder, Rabbit stopped to rest.

He sat with his back against a lone cottonwood tree, took a sip from his waterskin, and attempted to decide whether to dig for water here or to move on and search for water later. He rose to look around the area for a likely spot. There should be water available, since the cottonwood had seen many seasons here. He found a small depression with antelope and coyote tracks around the moist edges.

Dropping to his knees, Rabbit began to clean out and deepen the water hole. Idly, he wished the Blue Paints had done the work for him, as he had found on previous stops.

Suddenly he stopped short and leaped to his feet. Why hadn't they? Had he passed another water hole in the night? Was there another nearby?

He scrambled to the rim of the streambed for better visibility but saw no other watering place. Still his senses were reluctant to accept the inevitable fact that came rushing in on him. Those he followed had not been here.

Almost frantically, he searched for their trail, up and down the streambed and on both sides. There was not a single footprint except for his own and those of the wild creatures. Somewhere in the night, he had missed the tracks. The Blue Paints had turned from the stream to move in another direction.

Rabbit lost no time in starting on his back trail, mentally bewailing his poor judgment. He must quickly find the point where the others left the riverbed and follow them.

There was only one possible explanation. At some point they must have left this stream to push toward another water source, and they must have known where and when. To leave this source of water without being certain of the next would be suicide in this inhospitable country.

As he trotted, he tried to remember where the others might have changed direction. He dreaded the possibility that he was beginning to suspect. He was afraid that the night camp on the sandy streambed was in preparation for their change of course.

He could retrace his trail to that point, of course, and determine the new direction taken by the Blue Paints. The frustration came in the fact that while he had traveled so well, he actually had been losing time.

By the time he retraced his path to the ashes of the cold campfires, he would have lost an entire day's travel. Meanwhile, the strangers had pushed ahead, Rabbit reminded himself. Counting the day he had lost and the one they had gained, they were now two days farther ahead than ever.

He jogged on, trying to ignore the old hopeless feeling that was beginning to descend on him again.

10

» » »

His pace was much slower in the blistering sun, and he required more rest before he could rise and stagger on. Sun Boy was low on his homeward journey before Rabbit came to the abandoned camp. He sank to the ground, completely exhausted.

He could see the tracks quite plainly, turning northward as they left the streambed. For the hundredth time he berated himself for his stupidity.

By the time Rabbit was able to rise and stumble up the slope, twilight was falling. The trail lay invitingly before him, easy to follow, but he had learned his lesson. He would not attempt again to follow it in the darkness. He retraced his steps to the sandy streambed and methodically cleaned the seep spring left by the Blue Paints.

He drank long and filled his waterskin. He would drink again before morning and once more before he departed. The day ahead might be long and would certainly be dry.

Finally, with nothing to be accomplished before morning, Rabbit rolled in his robe and slept.

He was awakened by the distant boom of Rain Maker's drum and opened his eyes to the flash of real-fire in the

distance. Quickly, he leaped to his feet and began to
gather his few belongings.

Rabbit did not know this country, but the situation
was familiar, much like that in the land of the People.
Rain Maker would loose large quantities of water, flooding the dry watercourses. A surge of water could sweep
down the streambed, arriving even before the storm,
sometimes, from rains far upstream. It was not uncom-
mon for persons camped in such a location to be forced
to flee for their lives. Drownings were not unheard of.

The young man scrambled up the slope and looked for
a place to seek shelter. It must not be near a tree. Rain
Maker, with his perverse sense of humor, often enjoyed
driving people out of the low-lying places to seek shelter
under large trees. Then he would throw spears of real-fire
at the trees. His preference was for cottonwoods.

With this in mind, Rabbit sought a place beside a
rocky outcrop. It was above the stream's bed but not near
the highest points of land, those loved by Rain Maker's
real-fire. He squatted and spread his robe over his head to
await the passing of the storm.

Fat raindrops drummed on the taut skin of the robe,
then increased in volume as the full force of the storm
swept down. Rabbit tucked the robe around him and
waited. By the brief light of a flash of real-fire, he saw
water running down the center of the streambed in a
steady trickle. It seemed only a short while later that
another flash revealed the river nearly bank-full. Where
there had been the ashes of the Blue Paints' fires, there
was now only a swirling flood, sweeping along its own
debris. The stream's rise had been so swift that Rabbit
had a momentary urge to move to higher ground again.

Reason quickly returned, telling him that any flooding
beyond the bank-full level would be slow and deliberate.
He settled back again.

The storm lasted until just before morning. Rabbit
stood up and shook the water from his robe, waiting
eagerly for full daylight to allow better opportunity to
see his situation.

It was not good. The stream still ran nearly bank-full,
just beginning to drop a little. More important, Rabbit
now verified the thing he had feared through the long
night. He now had no trail to follow. All traces of the

tracks left by the Blue Paints were completely wiped clean. Now Rabbit had lost even his three-day-old trail. He had nothing at all to follow except a general direction. Even that was uncertain.

He looked at the slope and tried to remember where the trail had been, which way the tracks had pointed. It was useless. The entire landscape appeared different, washed by the night's rain. Even the colors had changed, the dull grays and browns of the plant life already showing new green.

Carefully, Rabbit reconsidered. The general direction of the stream they had been following was east and west, sometimes bending slightly north. At this point, there was a gentle westerly curve to the course they had followed, and it was at this point that the Blue Paints had left the stream. They had headed nearly straight north, from what he could remember of the tracks.

This must mean, Rabbit concluded, that there was another water source to the north, not more than a day's journey. Two, at most. It was probably a stream which ran parallel to this one. When the Blue Paints reached it, they would turn west again.

It was not so complicated. He must push as rapidly as possible to the north, trusting that the stream did exist. When he reached it, if there was no sign of those he sought, he would turn west again, or northwest. That was the direction of his original quest, he reminded himself.

Anyway, what choice did he have? He shouldered his pack and moved ahead.

By midday, he could see no sign of the rain that had fallen in an isolated area only. The sun now began to beat down on his head in earnest since the clouds had moved on. Rabbit began to have a gnawing doubt about his course of action. Was there really water ahead? He saw no fringe of willow to mark a watercourse, as far as the eye could see. Earth's rim, in the distance, looked as dry as the spot where he stood. Shimmering heat waves lent a ghostly air to the distant landscape.

Rabbit knew he must move on without pause. Survival depended on it. He tried not to think about the difference in a day's journey by horse, as the Blue Paints had, and on foot. His decision to head north may have been wrong. Doggedly, he plodded on.

Just before dark, he stopped in a small gully and attempted to dig for water. It was useless. After scooping sand for a while, he found only a hint of dampness at the bottom of the hole. He watched for some time, but there was no seep of water.

He rested for a while, then moved on. He realized that he must travel through the night to cover as much distance as possible before his strength was gone. Allowing himself only a sip of the water, which was becoming more precious, he slung the waterskin over his shoulder again and started forward, the Real-star pointing his direction.

He traveled steadily, pausing to rest only when he felt he must. By midmorning, he was staggering and falling. He used the last of his water.

Just after midday, Rabbit topped a low rise to see a lush green border of trees along the shore of a shimmering lake. He rushed forward, licking cracked lips in anticipation.

Suddenly the mirage disappeared in a wavering shift of air currents and rising heat waves. Ahead of him again was nothing but parched sand and stunted brush.

Aiee, it had been so real! He had heard of these glimpses into the Spirit World but had never seen one. What did it mean? Had he looked for a moment through a doorway into the Other Side?

He staggered on, becoming weaker and beginning to hallucinate. Sometimes he could not distinguish which was mirage and which was in his own head. Or did it really matter? Either was the doorway he sought to cross through. Perhaps they were the same.

Only one thing prevented him from loosening his grip on reality and giving way to his illusions. He had a mission.

Just now he couldn't remember what it was, but it was there. No matter how he wished to let go, to drift into the Spirit World, he must not. Not until he had accomplished whatever it was.

He sat down in the burning sand and stared at the illusion before him. It seemed so real, the feathery willows along a clear stream, only a bow shot away. It would vanish in a moment. He pushed away the temptation to rush forward and be tricked again. He would rest a little and move on.

Rabbit sank sideways, almost falling to a prone position. He must rest before he could even think any more.

A bow shot away, willows and cottonwoods stirred lazily in the summer breeze, and the stream murmured beneath their branches.

11

>> >> >>

Y ellow Bird and her friend, Pretty Basket, moved cautiously along the stream, searching for sand plums. There had been many plums this year. Their tribe had gathered large quantities to use immediately or to dry for storage. The people had eaten the tart fruit freely as they worked, and still their baskets were filled.

But now, the season was almost over. The fruit was becoming scarce. It was for this reason that the two girls had searched far downstream from the camp of their band. Farther than they should, both were well aware, with the Blue Paint People intruding into their country.

Perhaps it was this element of danger that intrigued them. Both were of marriageable age but were not yet spoken for. Thus their very eligibility made the danger exciting. They had giggled over secret conversations about it.

"What would you do, Yellow Bird, if you were carried off by the Blue Paints?"

Then both would giggle, excited and embarrassed. They had come to no reasonable conclusions.

Today, they wandered far downstream. There were few

plums, but they had enjoyed the privacy of their adventure, the occasional pause to wade in the stream. Now, it was time to return. Their families would become alarmed at their long absence.

"In a moment, Yellow Bird," pleaded Pretty Basket. "Let us look in that little clump near the hilltop. Then we will go."

In a way, this last look was a final flirt with danger. The scrubby thicket to which Pretty Basket pointed was some distance from the stream with its sheltering fringe of trees. They must cross an open area of a hundred paces or more in full view of any observer. Yellow Bird hesitated.

"I think not, Pretty Basket. It looks very dangerous."

"You are afraid," taunted her friend.

"No, I only think we should be cautious. You know there are Blue Paints in the area. They stole that girl from the Western band."

Pretty Basket rolled her eyes in mock alarm.

"Yes! What do you suppose happened to her?"

She paused, took a step or two into the open.

"Are you still afraid?"

Yellow Bird was caught between concern for her friend and her own intuition, which told her that this was no time for foolish things. Pretty Basket was now skipping up the slope, singing to herself. There was no time for thoughtful decisions.

"Wait," Yellow Bird called. She was irritated that her friend would put them both in danger in this way. Grumbling to herself, she started after the other girl. She had taken only a few steps when Pretty Basket came running down the slope, waving her arms and pointing.

"There is a dead warrior," she pointed frantically.

"One of ours?"

"No! A Blue Paint! Run!"

"Pretty Basket! Stop it! Tell me."

The two were running toward the shelter of the trees now, Pretty Basket babbling and crying. They reached concealment, and Yellow Bird seized her friend's arm roughly.

"Listen!" She snapped. "If the Blue Paints are here, there is no time to be foolish!"

For some time they crouched, listening and watching, but nothing happened.

"Where is your basket?" Yellow Bird demanded.

"I—I must have dropped it "

"We cannot leave it there. The enemy will find it and know we are near."

Pretty Basket was crying now, seemingly more concerned with her mother's anger over the loss of the basket.

"We must go and get it." Yellow Bird was firm.

"No, the warrior is there!"

"But he is dead. You told me. Come, show me where."

Cautiously, the two frightened girls crept back up the slope, hand in hand. Pretty Basket held back, attempting to hide behind her friend.

They rounded the shoulder of the little hillock and encountered the girl's basket, lying upside down where she had dropped it. A few plums lay scattered along the sand.

"There! There he is!" Pretty Basket pointed excitedly.

The body of a man lay a few steps away. He lay in a clumsy, contorted position, as if he had been struck down. Yellow Bird observed him carefully.

"I do not think he is a Blue Paint," she whispered.

"Yes, yes he is!"

"No. His hair is different. See, he parts it in the middle and binds each half down the sides. And, he wears no blue paint!"

Yellow Bird took another step to see more clearly. The man was young, little older than herself. She could see his sunburned face and blistered, cracked lips. He must have come across the Sand Hills, and probably on foot. Yes, she could see his staggering footprints in the sand where the man had crossed the last rise. He had not been dead long, because his body had not yet begun to bloat.

Strange, thought the girl. Why would this man cross the dry hills, come within sight of the river, and then lie down to die?

And who was he, from what strange tribe? How did he come to be on foot in the Sand Hills? There were many unanswered questions.

The girls crept closer, fascinated by the stranger who had apparently come so far to meet his fate. He wore a shirt and leggings of tanned skins, and on his feet were moccasins of unfamiliar pattern. An empty waterskin hung from his neck on a thong. No weapons were in evidence.

Yellow Bird was feeling sorrow for the man. How unfortunate to die so young and for no apparent purpose. She felt much as she had several seasons ago when she had found a dead fawn.

She had been gathering fuel near the camp of her band when she noticed the tiny thing curled beneath a bush. At first she had thought it was alive. It looked so perfectly formed, nothing unusual about the pretty spotted coat. The fawn had simply lain down to rest and never awakened. Such things were beyond understanding.

Now, as she recalled the fawn, her attention was brought suddenly back to the present. The stranger gave a long, shuddering sigh.

"Pretty Basket! He is alive!"

"Then we must kill him."

Pretty Basket was searching for a suitable stone to carry out her statement.

"No!" Yellow Bird almost screamed at the other girl. "He may be our friend!"

She was not certain why she felt the protective role. Perhaps it had something to do with the fawn. She had been able to do nothing to bring it back to life, but for this young man, there was another chance.

She lifted the empty waterskin from his neck and handed it to Pretty Basket.

"Go, bring some water."

The other girl was reluctant, but Yellow Bird was not to be argued with. Resignedly, Pretty Basket dropped her fist-sized stone.

"Yellow Bird," she warned, "he will do us harm."

"Nonsense! He cannot even hold his eyes open. Get the water!"

Yellow Bird straightened the cramped position of the man's limbs and gently brushed sand from his parched face. He moaned again, softly. He appeared very near death.

Pretty Basket returned, chattering her dire warnings like a squirrel scolding an intruder. Yellow Bird ignored her tirade but took the waterskin.

She poured a small amount of the precious fluid into her palm and held it to the man's face, bathing and

cooling the skin. He did not respond. Gently, she lifted
his head in her arm and trickled a few drops into his
mouth. At first there was no response, then the lips
parted and the tongue moved in a swallowing motion.

Yellow Bird turned to speak to her friend.

"Go, tell my father. He will bring a horse. Tell him we
will need a pole-drag."

"But, Yellow Bird—"

"Go!"

Pretty Basket turned and scampered away, muttering
to herself. Sometimes her friend could be so exasperating.

Yellow Bird settled to a more comfortable sitting position and lifted the head of the semiconscious man to her
lap. He would need much water, but scarcely a swallow
at a time at first. She dribbled a few drops between his
lips again, and he coughed for a moment, then opened
his mouth for more.

The girl began to croon gently to him, and he relaxed
in her arms. The words had no meaning to him, but the
tone was clear.

"Lie still and rest, my warrior. Drink slowly, until
your strength returns. I, Yellow Bird, will take care of
you."

She reached for the waterskin again and smiled to
herself. There was a strange thrill of excitement in the
responsibility she was undertaking.

12

>> >> >>

Rabbit lay comfortably, listening to the soft croon of his mother's voice. In his half-conscious state, it was so comforting to be held and rocked gently that he had no desire to awaken.

Water trickled between his dust-dry lips again, and he licked eagerly at it. Almost immediately he coughed, choking on the droplets that took the wrong path. His mother's arm cradled his head, assisting him to raise it for better breathing. He settled back, snuggled against the softness of her body, and breathed deeply again.

The comforting song continued in time to the gentle rocking motion. It was odd, Rabbit mused. He must have been very sick because he was having difficulty understanding the words of his mother's gentle lullaby.

He remembered the time that the People had camped near a swampy area. Evil spirits from the dark, foul-smelling waters had sickened many, both old and young, and some had died. Rabbit's own spirit had hovered for three suns, he had been told, undecided whether to cross over. Possibly it had been the stubbornness of his mother's will that had kept him alive. Willow had held and

rocked her feverish child, imparting her strength to him
as she sang softly.

Or was that this time? Was it now that he thought of,
instead of a dim memory? Tiredly, he struggled to understand the words of the soft lullaby. At first they seemed
to be the rhyming nonsense syllables of a child's song,
but one he had never heard. It was only gradually that it
came to him that the song was not in his own tongue.
The words were unfamiliar to him.

Alarmed, Rabbit opened his eyes and attempted to
focus on the face above him, swimming in and out of his
sight.

It was not his mother's face. It was that of a woman, a
beautiful young woman whom he had never seen before.
He had not understood her song because she sang in a
strange tongue. Frantically, Rabbit struggled to sit up but
fell back weakly.

"Lie still, rest a little."

He did not understand the words, but the girl accompanied them with sign talk. He glanced quickly around,
attempting to make sense out of this mystery.

The sight of the stream refreshed his memory. Ah yes!
He had crossed the dry hills, following the Blue Paints,
and had run out of water. It had been a very close escape.

Was the girl a Blue Paint? Was he a prisoner? He
looked sharply at her again. Surely not. She was near his
own age, and there was certainly nothing threatening
about her gentle smile. In fact, he thought it quite possibly the loveliest smile he had ever seen.

"Who are you?" he motioned in sign talk. "What is
your tribe?"

"I am Yellow Bird. Mine are the People."

There was a moment of confusion. The girl had accompanied her sign for "people" with a spoken name
which was unfamiliar to Rabbit. Then it became clear to
him. Most tribes' names for themselves could be interpreted as "the People." He smiled.

"My people also call themselves the People," he signed.
Both chuckled at his different word with the same
meaning.

"Sometimes," he added, "we are called Elk-dog People."

He attempted again to sit up and this time was able to
do so with the girl's help. He was feeling much better

but still very weak. She continued to support him to prevent his toppling over again.

Finally, he seemed stable enough for her to free her hands for sign talk.

"How are you called?" she asked.

Rabbit very nearly gave himself away. He was so relaxed and confident with this young woman that he almost gave the sign for "rabbit." But this would never do. How could he call the attention of this, the most beautiful of women, to his too-prominent teeth? She had probably already noticed. Self-consciously, his hand strayed to his mouth.

Then he assumed what he hoped would be a stern and confident expression.

"I am called Horse Seeker," he signaled. "I follow a vision quest."

"Horse Seeker" neglected to mention that he had completely failed in his quest, lost his horse, equipment, and the sacred elk-dog medicine of the People. Somehow none of these things seemed urgent at all when compared to the inspiration of Yellow Bird's smile.

"What were you doing in the Sand Hills?"

"I was following my enemy. They wear blue face paint."

He was talking too much, he realized. This girl might be a friend or ally of those he followed, possibly one of them herself. He would be more careful.

But the girl was nodding eagerly.

"The Blue Paints! Yes, they are our enemies, too!"

Rabbit felt somewhat better. He did not fail to notice, however, the quick glance around and the look of fear on the girl's face. Something stirred in his memory. He had experienced this smell of fear before, but he could not quite identify it.

"Look!" Yellow Bird stood and pointed. "My people come!"

Rabbit, now Horse Seeker, attempted to rise but fell back weakly on the sand. He simply had not the strength.

Yellow Bird was beside him in an instant, supporting, helping, crooning words of comfort.

A group of perhaps a dozen people straggled over a rise from upriver somewhere. Yellow Bird waved and called out. Two young men rode forward on horseback, weapons at the ready, circling suspiciously. The young woman

spoke sharply to them, and they relaxed somewhat, coming forward to dismount.

The rest of the party now approached on foot, also
heavily armed. A young woman led them, pointing and
talking at a rapid rate. She was about the age of Yellow
Bird, Horse Seeker thought, but not nearly so pretty.

A middle-aged warrior led a horse with a pole-drag
much like those used by the People. From the way they
greeted each other, Horse Seeker guessed that this must
be the father of Yellow Bird. The man's demeanor further
identified him as a leader, probably a respected subchief.

Horse Seeker was keenly aware of the rules of protocol. A visitor must pay his respects to the chief of the
host tribe. If he could not stand, at least he could observe
the formalities.

"Greetings, my chief," he signed. "I am Horse Seeker,
of the Elk-dog People."

He pointed to the southeast.

The other man nodded.

"I know. Come."

He motioned to the pole-drag. Horse Seeker realized
that the girl must have told her father the rudiments of
the situation at first greeting.

The other members of the party cast anxious glances
around the landscape. Yellow Bird beckoned again and
assisted him to rise on shaky legs. It was only a step or
two, but it required every bit of strength that he could
muster. Horse Seeker nearly fell before Yellow Bird and
her father were able to help him to a reclining position
on the pole-drag.

Immediately the party set out at a fast walk, upstream.
The invalid was jolted on the pole-drag behind the horse
in what he believed to be the roughest ride of his life.

Shadows were growing long by the time they reached a
village of lodges much like those of the People. Children
and dogs ran alongside the drag, curious and noisy. They
wound their way among the lodges and stopped in front
of a large dwelling.

"Welcome to my lodge," signed the father of Yellow
Bird.

The young man nodded weakly. It had been a grueling
trip. Still, he had been aware enough to observe one
inescapable fact. All the people he had seen had seemed

timid and afraid, casting anxious glances at every bush and rock.

Even the subchief himself, beneath his dignified demeanor, had seemed eager to reach the comparative safety of the village. Something was wrong, permeating the entire village, perhaps the whole tribe.

As they helped him into the lodge, to the welcome luxury of a soft pallet of robes, Horse Seeker was puzzling over the mystery of the thing.

What was going on?

13

>> >> >>

It was not long before Rabbit, now Horse Seeker, learned
the reasons for the sense of fear that lay heavily over the
tribe of Yellow Bird.

He had recovered rapidly from his close encounter
with the Spirit World and had begun to learn things
about his hosts and their customs. He remained a guest
in the lodge of Spotted Elk and Bright Leaf, parents of the
girl.

Yellow Bird's people, he had been informed, were sometimes known to other tribes as the River People. Horse
Seeker was surprised to learn the origin of the name.
Until a generation ago, the tribe had been growers, living
along the river valleys of this portion of the plains. They
had lived much as had the Growers of his own area, in
semipermanent villages near their crops, trading with
the hunting tribes for meat and robes.

All this had changed abruptly with the acquisition of
the horse. Young men were no longer willing to cultivate
corn and pumpkins when they could ride like the wind
in pursuit of buffalo. In the space of a few seasons, the
River People had moved away from the watercourses,

out onto the plain, following the herds. They had adopted the conical skin lodges of the hunting tribes and successfully competed for a place in the prairie.

But this had not been without problems. The River People were, by tradition, nonaggressors, trading with all comers. Now, the hunters saw them as intruders into the hunting grounds and reacted with force. It was with some difficulty that the River People were able to react and defend themselves. Still, there had been no thought of returning to their former way of life.

In the ensuing generation, their relationship with the hunters had stabilized to a place somewhere between armed truce and open warfare. Still, it was claimed, the River People had never been the aggressors.

The worst of their enemies were the fierce and warlike Blue Paints, Horse Seeker was told. This tribe was originally from farther north but had drifted into the area in the past few generations. They were aggressive, ruthless, and hated all the more because they had no real claim to this territory at all. Their unpredictability presented a constant source of haunting fear for the River People.

All these things Horse Seeker learned gradually, as he learned the language. The tongue of the River People was completely different from his own, but with the help of the sign talk, he was mastering it rapidly.

He told his hosts of his own tribe, of their customs, their origins, and of his grandfather and the First Elk-dog.

Some things he omitted. It would be embarrassing to let it be known that he was a medicine man whose powers were so insignificant that he had failed in his vision quest and lost the strongest medicine of his tribe. It was much like his reasons for calling himself Horse Seeker instead of the childish appellation Rabbit.

He participated in the hunt, after his strength returned, as was considered proper for a guest, to help contribute to his keep. His ability with the horse was recognized by these, a people with a generation less experience than his own. He was quickly accepted by those his own age.

Through all this period of his recovery, Horse Seeker gave little thought to anything but the day at hand. It was pleasant, in the long warm days of the Moon of Ripening, to hunt with the other young men, to exchange stories with the older members of the band around the lodge fires in the chill of evening.

Perhaps most important was the presence of the girl. Yellow Bird had assumed a possessive attitude that plainly said the stranger belonged to her. Horse Seeker felt this keenly. At first, it seemed only the logical concern for one whose life she had saved. It became apparent, however, that the girl saw more in the relationship than this. Her approach was one of fierce protection, which manifested itself in odd ways. Yellow Bird seemed possessed with the necessity to do all she could for him

She brought him the choicest of food, the coolest of water to drink. As he became more ambulatory, she had shown him around the camp, introduced him to her friends, and taken him to her favorite places.

The members of the band good-naturedly smiled and accepted him as Yellow Bird's stranger from a far tribe. There were only a few resentful glances by young men who might have sought her for themselves.

Horse Seeker was enjoying the attention. At first he was grateful for the girl's role in saving his life, but it soon became more than that. She was pleasant to be with. They laughed and talked as she helped his halting efforts to learn her language.

It was very easy to spend his days with Yellow Bird and to forget that there had ever been another life. He thought less and less about his own tribe, his family, and the responsibilities he had left behind. Someday he must think and plan, decide how to seek the return of the elk-dog medicine.

Yet it was so easy to postpone such serious things. Again and again he made private excuses, telling himself he would surely make decisions next day to begin to resume his quest.

Then Yellow Bird would come to him, take his hand, and lead him to some secluded spot where they could sit beside the stream in the warm autumn sunlight. They would watch quiet ripples in the smooth water made by a brood of ducklings as they followed their mother along the far shore. Soon the birds would be mature enough to wing south for the winter.

Thinking about the winter made the young man uneasy. Just as there was little time for the ducklings to

mature and gain strength for their long journey, there
was very little time for him to make decisions. Soon the
onslaught of Cold Maker would sweep across the prairie,
making travel impractical for several moons. Even worse,
he was unfamiliar with this country. What sort of winter
would it be? He could only guess.

He was afraid it would be harsh. He had traveled some
distance north on his mission, nearer to the traditional
abode of Cold Maker.

Well, what did it matter? How could he travel, anyway? He had no horse, no weapons, and no clear idea
where he should go. He could not return to his own
people until he had somehow overcome his failures. And
how could he plan that, with winter nearly upon him?

He attempted to ignore the major reason for his reluc-
tance. It was simply more pleasant to stay in the relative
security of the River People's camp, enjoying good food,
warmth, shelter, and the company of the girl who had so
rapidly become the most important thing in his life.

Yes, surely the most expedient plan was to spend the
winter with Yellow Bird's people.

14

» » »

Spotted Elk was uneasy about his guest. Initially, he had had a great sense of pride in his daughter for her part in saving the young man's life. It was good to have another warrior to join them. It might be very beneficial, in the event of an attack by the Blue Paints, to have another fighting man.

However, there were certain doubts in the heart of the band chief. Spotted Elk had never been exactly certain as to the reasons for this Horse Seeker to be where they had found him. *Why* had he been there? The stranger had been on foot in an area where no one travels on foot. He was unarmed where one always carries weapons.

True, Horse Seeker had explained that he had been set upon by the Blue Paints, but his explanation was very sketchy. True, the enemy may have taken his horse and his weapons, but why had they not killed him? And again, what was the young man doing so far from his tribe?

Spotted Elk would never have pried into the answers to these questions. It would have been extremely impolite to question a guest in one's lodge. These things were private matters of Horse Seeker's. He could tell, or not, as he chose. And there was much, Spotted Elk feared, that the young man chose not to reveal.

He wanted to like this young man. He had been impressed by the rapid manner in which Horse Seeker had started to learn the language of the River People. The young man seemed appreciative for the help he had been given. No sooner had Horse Seeker regained his strength than he had participated in the hunt. Those who watched told of his skill with elk-dogs and that he hunted well. The young men seemed to accept the stranger, and he was becoming well liked, except for a few. There were those prospective suitors of Yellow Bird who resented his coming.

Reluctantly, Spotted Elk had to admit that perhaps they and he suffered from the same doubts. Here was this handsome young outsider who seemed honest and sincere. He was well liked, capable, and intelligent, but his background was unknown. Spotted Elk resented the interest shown by Yellow Bird and the threat that the stranger represented to his family.

Once he cautioned the girl about it.

"Daughter, you are not his mother. Do not hover over this man. You know nothing about him."

The dark eyes flashed fire.

"I found him. I will treat him as I please!"

Spotted Elk sighed and dropped the conversation. He could not fight this in his daughter.

All her life she had brought sick and injured creatures into his lodge. How like her mother, he used to think, watching her feed a baby bird or comfort a puppy with a broken leg. But, never before had she gone this far. He had never expected to have her drag home a prospective husband. If only she would show this much interest in some of the young men of her own tribe. He could think of several whose families owned many horses and comfortable lodges. He sighed again.

A chill breeze crept around the doorway, and Spotted Elk drew his robe around his legs. It would soon be winter. The band should move to winter camp. It would take several sleeps to reach the area where they customarily wintered, and it was time to start.

Suddenly a thought came to him. Good! It might be

possible to accomplish two things at once. Elated at his idea, Spotted Elk almost sprang to his feet and left the lodge, while Bright Leaf stared after him in surprise.

He did not know where the young people might have gone. He searched at random for a time and at last encountered Pretty Basket, who greeted him cheerfully. After polite conversation, Spotted Elk came to his question.

"Have you seen Horse Seeker?"

The girl giggled and nodded.

"Yellow Bird took him to walk along the stream."

"Where?"

"That way."

How could everyone take such great pleasure in this friendship, he asked himself as he strode purposefully upstream.

It was no matter now, however. He thought that he had solved his problem. He would move the band into winter camp, further away from Horse Seeker's people. This would force the young man into a decision.

Now he saw the young couple coming toward him along the stream, hand in hand. Yellow Bird chattered happily, looking into the face of Horse Seeker with adoration. Her father winced, then contained his feelings and waved a greeting to them.

"Yellow Bird," he began after the initial greeting, "you go on. I would talk with Horse Seeker."

The two men walked for a moment in silence, then the chief spoke.

"Horse Seeker, the time has come for my people to move."

"Yes?"

"We go west, into the hills below the mountains, to camp for the winter."

Horse Seeker still showed no signs of understanding, so the other repeated, using hand talk also.

The young man nodded.

"Yes, I understand."

"You will not wish to go farther from your tribe. Or, you may wish to continue your journey."

It was a question, rather than a statement, but Spotted Elk continued.

"I will give you a horse and weapons, and you can do as you wish."

Spotted Elk felt a great sense of satisfaction at his own cleverness. It was a good exchange, a horse and weapons to be rid of the uneasy feelings he felt about the mysterious stranger from far away.

But now, the young man was answering. He spoke fairly well for someone just learning the language, and he also used hand signs.

"You will travel for many sleeps?"

Spotted Horse nodded.

"There will be some dangers? Maybe the Blue Paints?"

Again, the chief nodded, puzzled. He did not understand where this conversation was going.

"Then I must go with you. You may need another warrior."

Before the astonished Spotted Elk could answer, the young man continued.

"You have already been so helpful to me, Uncle, I could not take the horse. I owe you at least this, to help your people against the Blue Paints. But, I would welcome the use of a bow."

Spotted Elk walked along in silence. How had this happened? This was not the expected result. He had thought that his offer would remove his worries. Instead, the realization was sinking into his heart that now the young man was to be his guest for the winter.

Even more frustrating, somehow he now felt that he should thank the young stranger for staying in his lodge to help with its defense.

15

>> >> >>

It was only three suns later that Spotted Elk moved his band.

To Horse Seeker, it was a familiar scene. Lodge covers were folded and bundled, possessions stowed in rawhide packs. Lodge poles were taken down, some to be used as pole-drags to carry the heavy skin covers. Other poles were tied loosely together merely to transport them.

The importance of the lodge poles was plain. Wood for straight, slim poles was scarce on the high prairie. Horse Seeker noted that the poles were of different wood than those of his own tribe. These slim poles were of pine, probably a special sort. He recalled that the Red Rocks band of the People sometimes acquired pine poles in their semimountainous area.

Aiee, he thought, a tribe's way of living is patterned by where they live. His father, Owl, who had traveled far, had told him of this from his own experience, but Horse Seeker had only now begun to see it firsthand.

Then another thought occurred to him. Spotted Elk had mentioned mountains. There had been mountains in his dream. For a moment, Horse Seeker had a strange sensation that he had lived all this before. His heart jumped with excitement. He felt that he was once again moving in the direction of fulfillment of his vision quest. He tried not to think of the utter frustration and futility that had followed him.

His spirits were further lifted as the River People fell into line to travel. A crow in a cottonwood thicket flared up in alarm, cawing loudly. The bird circled once, over the travelers, and swooped close to Horse Seeker. Once more, he was startled when the crow looked directly into his eyes and he recognized his medicine guide.

It was only for the space of a heartbeat that the shiny eye looked into his, no, *through* his eyes, to speak to his very spirit. Then the bird uttered three raucous cries and flew straightaway to the northwest.

The northwest! The hair prickled on the back of Horse Seeker's neck. It had been long since he felt this thrill of excitement, the urge to be on his quest. He touched heels to the flanks of his borrowed horse and moved forward to ride beside Yellow Bird's father. He felt better than at any time since he joined these people.

It was on the third day of travel that the advance scouts signaled the approach of other riders. For a moment, Horse Seeker thought there would be panic. People milled around excitedly. And fearfully, he noted. There it was again, the unreasoning smell of fear, so much a part of these people's lives.

He did not understand it. The approach of riders should signify little danger. Even if they were enemy warriors, on a hunt or a war party, they would not attack the entire band.

The other possibility seemed even more unlikely to cause danger. In his own country, bands on the move frequently encountered bands from other tribes. It was customary to pause for the chiefs to exchange greetings, even though they might be enemies. Neither would wish conflict with the women and children present. It could become too dangerous.

So, when Horse Seeker's own people met a band of Head Splitters while on the move, there would be mild insults, exaggerated threats, and good-natured banter. This, however, between men who would fight to kill at their next meeting.

The young man relaxed on his horse, expecting this

sort of encounter. The others huddled together, wary and
apprehensive. Spotted Elk did not ride out to meet the
approaching horsemen but stationed himself near the
others.

Soon a column of riders approached over a distant rise.
It was apparent that this was, indeed, a band of families
on the move. Heavily laden pole-drags were in evidence,
as well as women and children on foot. Good. There
would be no trouble at all, Horse Seeker told himself.

As the strangers approached several of their warriors
detached themselves from the group and rode forward at
a lope. Horse Seeker wondered why Spotted Elk's people
did not advance a similar delegation. It would have been
customary in his own country.

"The Blue Paints," someone whispered.

Suddenly, he recognized the gray horse ridden by one
of the strangers. Yes, there was no doubt. He could never
forget the proud carriage, the look of eagles in the eye of
Gray Cloud. The man who rode her was the same burly
chief he had met before.

"That is Walks-Like-Thunder," Yellow Bird whispered
in his ear. "He is the worst of all the Blue Paints."

Horse Seeker nodded.

"Yes," he muttered bitterly. "We have met. That is my
horse."

The enemy warriors arrogantly rode among the cower-
ing River People. Everyone stood very still, anxious not
to provoke overt action. The riders peered and poked
among the baggage, looting a few small articles and pieces
of dried meat or other foodstuffs.

Horse Seeker was aghast, both at the arrogance of the
Blue Paints and the fact that the River People would
tolerate such an affront. He glanced around, but no one
seemed willing to risk the anger of the strangers. His
frustration mounted.

Soon the intruders tired of this amusement and gathered as a group to confront Spotted Elk and his warriors.

"Greetings, my chief!"

Walks-Like-Thunder sneered as he made the hand signs
with an exaggerated politeness and deference.

"Greetings," replied Spotted Elk, carefully. "It is well
with you?"

"Of course. It is always well with us."

His expression was taunting. Then he noticed Horse Seeker, sitting on his horse behind the chiefs.

"Who is this?" the Blue Paint signed in amazement.

His next message was directed to the young man.

"How is it that you are here? We killed you once."

There was a ripple of laughter from his followers.

"You would hide for protection among these?"

He gazed at Spotted Elk's warriors in mock amazement.

Horse Seeker recognized the game. His people were adept at it. Taunts were exchanged with the chance that someone would lose his temper and act out of anger instead of judgment. The object was to tread the fine edge of the opponent's temper, to goad him almost to the point of rage, but not quite.

But Spotted Elk's warriors made no retort to the Blue Paint's sidelong slur at their manhood. Astonished, Horse Seeker rose to his own defense.

"I hide from no one. I did not leave our fight. You did!"

There was a gasp from some of Spotted Elk's warriors who did not understand this exchange. Spotted Elk was staring.

The Blue Paint leader chuckled aloud.

"You were not able to leave!"

"But I am here."

"Yes," the other acknowledged. "But I have forgotten— how are you called? Horse Seeker? Did you find your horse?"

The other Blue Paints rocked with laughter.

"I never lost her. I will take her back someday."

The River People were astounded at his boast. Some fingered their weapons and cast anxious glances at their chief.

The big Blue Paint leader leaned forward to taunt.

"You wish to try now, Horse Seeker? I will kill you again."

As he moved, sunlight sparkled from a shiny object on his chest.

The Spanish bit swung gently on its thong. Horse Seeker swallowed hard, controlled his anger, and spoke.

"And my medicine will kill you!"

He pointed to the sacred object of the People, then continued.

"Even if you kill me, you are dying. Stolen medicine works against the thief!"

Walks-Like-Thunder looked doubtful for only a moment, then laughed a little nervously.

"It is not true! I am strong, and I will kill you!"

Trying to appear as calm as he could, Horse Seeker shrugged. The other was on the defensive.

"You are much like your name," the young man observed casually. "Thunder makes much noise but does little damage."

With a great show of confidence, he reined the horse and deliberately turned his back on the Blue Pints.

The burly chief was livid with rage and reached for a weapon, but a firm voice broke the stunned silence.

"Stop!"

Spotted Elk's command caused all to turn. Events had now progressed to the point where he was experienced. When the River People had lived in their permanent villages, they had traded with all.

By common consent, it was understood that out of courtesy to the host tribe, enemies who met in the course of their trading would not fight. Spotted Elk saw a similarity in the present situation.

"Stop! You have no regard for courtesy, Walks-Like-Thunder, to threaten harm to my guest!"

The other River People were now astonished at their chief. None of their tribe had ever dared talk so to the more powerful Blue Paints.

For a moment, it looked as though Walks-Like-Thunder would strike out at Spotted Elk. Then he slowly turned back to Horse Seeker.

"When we meet again, we will fight," he formed the hand signs deliberately. "I will kill you."

Horse Seeker said nothing. He had pushed the man dangerously. There was a hot temper there, which might prove useful someday. For it was becoming more apparent that someday he would have to fight the big man.

It had been only talk, the talk of the elk-dog medicine's power. It was powerful, yes, but for controlling elk-dogs, not for killing enemies. Horse Seeker had merely wished to plant the seed of doubt. If Walks-Like-Thunder was worrying a little about the power of stolen medicine, he would not be so alert.

The Blue Paints were leaving now, contenting themselves with a few obscene gestures as they departed. The River People relaxed and prepared to move on. Spotted Elk and Horse Seeker found themselves almost heroes for having stood up to the Blue Paints.

"Thank you, my chief. You saved me from a blow to the back."

"It was nothing, Horse Seeker. He broke the rules of hospitality."

Spotted Elk paused and gave a long sigh.

"I am afraid you made a powerful enemy today."

"No, my chief. This man was already my enemy. He rides my horse and wears the medicine of my people."

16

>> >> >>

Winter came early. Yellow Bird's people had scarcely established their camp in a sheltered valley under the mountains.

It was the Moon of Falling Leaves, and the cottonwood trees painted themselves the brightest of yellows before fluttering to the ground. Long lines of geese honked their way south, and the horses began to appear furry in their winter coats.

A thin haze hung over the world, deepening the misty blue of the distant peaks. Horse Seeker had been surprised at his first sight of the mountains. For most of a day's travel he had watched a distant cloud bank, becoming anxious over the threat of a storm. He was doubly concerned that none of his companions seemed to even notice. What sort of people were these, to ignore the signs of threatening weather?

His alarm turned to embarrassment when he realized, late in the day, that the dim blue line to the northwest was not a storm front but a range of mountains. *Aiee*, it was good that he had said nothing! He attempted to behave as if he had seen mountains many times.

Even so, his heart leaped at the sight. Again, he felt closer to his vision quest. With a thrill, he told himself that the blue shapes in the distance appeared much like those in his dream.

The valley chosen by Spotted Elk's band was well protected from the elements. To the north and west, a thin growth of pines clothed the slope, slowing the thrust of the winds. The woods would also act to catch and hold driven snow, sheltering the camp from deep drifting.

Each family worked to make its lodge ready for winter. Dry grass was stuffed inside the lodge linings. A barrier of brush and pine boughs was built to the north of some dwellings to protect against the force of the wind. One man even extended the windbreak completely around his lodge, forming an enclosure for his most prized buffalo horse.

Horse Seeker helped in the winterizing of his host's lodge. He was completely familiar with the procedure, much like that of his own people.

It was to be expected that a time of warm, sunny days would follow. Sun Boy would gradually carry his torch more to the south on his daily run. Horse Seeker had wondered if Sun Boy did so in an attempt to follow the wild geese.

Whatever the reason, the result was the same every year. As Sun Boy's run became shorter, his torch weakened, and Cold Maker would take advantage of the situation. He would come roaring out of his home in the northern mountains to strike the prairie with his wrath.

This year was no exception, except that Cold Maker acted with more cunning than usual. His brother, Rain Maker, acted first to dampen Sun Boy's torch. For three days the world was damp, soggy, and cool. Sun Boy was not even seen.

Finally a few pale yellow rays managed to pierce the gray clouds, promising a return to the warm, pungent-smelling days of autumn. But it was not to be.

That night Cold Maker crept down from his lodge in the north. He did not bluster and howl and threaten, as he sometimes did. Instead, he crept quietly across the land, spreading a furry thin robe of frost over all. Those trees in sheltered places which still showed the green of growing life were blackened by Cold Maker's death stroke.

Children at play, pretending the customs of their el-
ders, blew clouds of smokelike breath from their council
pipes to sparkle for a moment in the still, frosty air. The
dogs and horses humped their backs against the cold,
shivering as they turned, attempting to warm themselves
by the rays of Sun Boy's torch.

By midday it was still, gray, and cloudy again. Rain
began to fall in a fine mist, freezing as it fell, to coat the
world in glistening ice. The River People retreated inside
their lodges.

Toward evening, Horse Seeker stepped outside to relieve the fullness in his bladder and found that the rain
had turned to snow. Fluffy, soft feathers of delicate white
settled quietly on the world in an unending supply. The
pines behind the camp were not even visible, and the
ground was already white. Horses stood motionless while
a robe of snow gathered and thickened on each furry
back. There was something eerie about the chill silence,
and Horse Seeker was glad to return to the warmth of the
lodge.

There were, later, some warm sunny days, but this
quiet snow marked the onset of Cold Maker's yearly
reign. Fortunately, there was enough food.

Snow drifted deeply around the lodges to remain most
of the season. The horses became thin, foraging among
the trees along the stream and subsisting mostly on cottonwood twigs and bark as winter continued.

Of course, winter had its rewards, also. There came to
be beaten paths in the snow, crisscrossing and connect-
ing the lodges, the stream, and the woods, their source of
fuel.

During many long evenings, friends would gather to
smoke, talk, gamble with the game sticks or plum stones,
or exchange stories. One of the favorite gathering places
was the lodge of Spotted Elk. It was good to have an
outsider in their midst to tell stories new to this tribe.

Horse Seeker was questioned many times about the
customs of his people, their traditions and legends. He
recounted the creation story of the People, how the Old
Man of the Shadows sat astride a hollow log tapping
with a drumstick. With each tap, another of the People
emerged from inside the earth by crawling through the
log.

Horse Seeker was an able storyteller and had heard this and the other tales of the Old Man since childhood. Usually it had been from the lips of his uncle, Eagle, who was felt to have mystical knowledge beyond most. At any rate, his stories could cause the neck hairs to prickle and the listener to edge closer to the fire.

The young man tried his best to imitate Eagle's style and manner. What he lacked in experience with the River People's language, he made up by the use of sign talk. He acted the parts of each individual in the stories he told.

Horse Seeker became more and more popular among the River People. This was a welcome respite from the monotony of the Moon of Long Nights and the Moon of Snows. By the Moon of Hunger, he was considered a part of the band.

The Moon of Hunger, of course, was now a misnomer. Since the coming of the horse, it had become so much easier to kill buffalo that there was seldom the starvation remembered by the old ones. Horse Seeker recounted to them that his own people joked about finding a new name for the Moon of Hunger.

Still, it was always with some relief that Sun Boy began to return, his torch replenished and brightening. Everyone had much more confidence when the Moon of Awakening returned.

It had not been an unpleasant winter. Horse Seeker had enjoyed the honor of entertaining these kind people. He had become almost inseparable from Yellow Bird. To most of the band, it was an accepted fact that the two were as one.

Only Spotted Elk still had reservations. He found it impossible to dislike this amusing young man. Yet there were still unanswered questions which he could not ask.

Above all, the threat which bothered him most was that he might lose his only daughter to this outsider, who would take her far away.

17
» » »

It was the Moon of Greening. Even in this semiarid country, the melting snows and warm rains caused the coming of new growth to the hills and valleys. It was as though the gray-brown vegetation had lain in wait for the right moment. Then, with the odor of damp earth everywhere, the rejuvenation took place.

Herds of buffalo suddenly appeared from the south, following the course of the wild geese overhead. The first herds were small and scattered, certainly not the huge numbers of the grasslands farther to the east. But they kept coming, by twos and threes, then by handfuls, then by hundreds.

The hunters were busy. In some seasons, Horse Seeker was told, buffalo were scarce. It was necessary to move out onto the plains by this time of the year. This season appeared exceptionally good. There was no need to move yet. Yellow Bird's people were content, the children fat and the women happy.

Horse Seeker participated in the hunting. He was well liked, respected for his abilities and his sense of humor. On borrowed horses belonging to Spotted Elk, he demonstrated his hunting skills repeatedly. Even when his luck was poor, however, his readiness to laugh at himself increased his popularity.

The primary quality which the young people of the band respected, however, was the visitor's skill with horses. It was said that no one could see inside the head of an elk-dog like Horse Seeker. He seemed able to talk to the animals.

"I see why you are called Horse Seeker," a young man remarked to him after an especially successful hunt.

Horse Seeker, who should have felt pleased by the compliment, was depressed. It was a reminder of failure. He felt that he was under false pretense, enjoying himself here among these hospitable people rather than pursuing his mission.

Even his assumed name bothered him. Why had he told such an untruth? He was merely a young apprentice medicine man named Rabbit, from a tribe far away. He could not have explained why it bothered him to have the respect offered by his new friends. He did not understand it himself.

Neither did he quite know why he had kept silent about his status as a medicine man. Perhaps he felt that, if it were known, he must make good on his quest and on the recovery of the elk-dog medicine amulet. And, so far, he had to admit that he had no idea whatever where to begin.

Then came a fateful day, a turning point. Horse Seeker and a few others of the young men had taken a hunt to the north. There was no actual need to go so far, as there were buffalo nearer to camp.

But it was spring, the young men were restless, and it seemed a good thing. They would travel a full sun, then hunt and explore another before returning on the third day. Black Otter and Lean Elk had promised to show the visitor an excitingly beautiful area. Horse Seeker had consented with only a twinge of conscience, which nagged at him to pay attention to his mission. It was far easier to think about an enjoyable hunting trip.

The hunters reached the area of the first night's camp well before Sun Boy retired to his lodge. They explored the area, backed off hastily from a chance encounter

with a real-bear and her cubs, and finally settled down
for the night.

The stars seemed close enough to touch, in the clear
mountain air, and the young men stayed awake a long
time, exchanging stories. They watched the Seven Hunters wheel their great circle in the sky around their camp
at the Real-star.

Once, they heard the nicker of a horse in the distance.
Someone went to check on their own animals and returned to report that all was well. It was probably a wild
elk-dog, someone said. There were known to be many in
the area.

Still, the mood of the party had changed. There was
the slight weight of doubt now, casting a cloud over their
happy air of unconcern. Conversation lagged, and finally
they sought their robes one by one, leaving one of their
number as a sentry.

Daylight seemed to arrive only moments later, and
the hunters rose to greet the warming rays of the sun. The
gloom of the time of darkness was gone, banished by the
beauty of the morning.

A doe with a tiny fawn tiptoed down to the stream to
drink. Birds sang in the thickets along the bank.

A crow called loudly from the top of a lone cottonwood, attracting Horse Seeker's attention. He was just
fastening his gaze on the creature, suspecting that it
might be his spirit-guide, when someone spoke to him,
distracting his thoughts. When he looked back, the bird
was gone.

Still, Horse Seeker felt that there was something unique
and special about the day, a thrill of excitement in the
air. His mood was heightened by a chance remark from
Black Otter.

"Today, Horse Seeker, you will not need to seek. We
will show you horses! We will return by a different
way."

They ate, mounted, and headed southwest. Very soon,
they approached a low ridge and spread out with caution
while one man carefully crept to the top. It would be
foolhardy to ride into an area without a precautionary
look.

The scout peered over the crest, then slid back a step
or two and beckoned excitedly. The others pressed for-

ward, bending low to keep out of sight until they knew the situation.

"Elk-dogs!" the young man whispered excitedly. "There are many!"

It was true, Across the green expanse of the little valley were scattered horses of all sizes and colors. Mares heavy in foal nibbled hungrily at the new grass. Tiny colts tottered clumsily around their protective dams. A couple of young stallions squared off in mock combat, squealing and striking. The watchers were enthralled by the scene.

"Aiee!" Horse Seeker muttered to himself. He was impressed not so much by the numbers of horses that he saw, only some thirty or forty. It was their quality.

His people had possessed the elk-dog for many summers, starting with the First Elk-dog of his grandfather. That one, Heads Off had stated many times, was of the finest blood from his own land, far across the Big Water.

There had been influxes of other breeding, also. Some animals had been captured from settlements of the Hairfaces far to the southwest. Still others had been brought by the expedition searching for the lost young officer, Juan Garcia, who was now Heads Off of the Elk-dog People.

Yes, the People knew horses well. The elk-dog had become a very important part of their lives. And, Horse Seeker had to admit, he had never seen animals of better quality. He singled out several mares which would compare favorably with the finest stock of the People.

"Let us try to catch some horses!" he whispered excitedly to Black Otter.

The other nodded.

"We can come up through the gully on the east and cut off part of the herd."

It was quickly planned. Horse Seeker and two more would stay hidden and watch.

The others retreated, circled, and as rapidly as was practical approached the valley from the hidden ravine. When they began their charge, Horse Seeker and his companions would ride in from the south, catching a portion of the animals between them. If they could herd some into a circling group, they might capture selected animals.

Horse Seeker shook out his rawhide rope. There were only two ropes in the party, but it mattered little. The day was one more of fun and relaxation than of serious horse hunting.

One red roan mare, who appeared to be the leader of the horse band, was becoming suspicious. She raised her head, ears erect and with nostrils testing the wind. A strong, straight-legged foal at her flank nickered a shrill question. Horse Seeker decided that he would try for the roan's colt.

Now Black Otter and the others kneed their mounts out into the open. The wild horses, alarmed, began to run, only to see Horse Seeker and his companions charge at them from another angle. Confused, the animals began to circle, pressing up the steep slope toward the rim of the valley.

Horse Seeker, his rope ready, attempted to craw along-side the roan mare. Her colt kept darting to the far side, hiding behind his mother no matter how the rider approached.

Perhaps he could catch the mare, the young man thought desperately. Then he would have both.

But they were nearing the valley's rim. The mare clattered across loose rimrock, straining to reach the top.

From the corner of his eye, Horse Seeker saw one of his companions pushing to turn a young mare aside before they reached the top.

Suddenly, from somewhere above them came the shrill sound of a stallion's call. The horses paused in confusion, and the roan mare answered in the moment of silence, a squeal of desperation.

The stallion seemed to come from nowhere. One moment there was nothing there, and a heartbeat later he loomed above them. The great red animal reared on hind legs, almost within striking distance of one of the riders. The ears were flattened, teeth bared, and the eyes seemed to flash fire. The rider flung himself backward from his horse in terror and scrambled down the slope toward the safety of some jumbled boulders.

The stallion screamed again, and the other riders stared in awe at his size, strength, and beauty. The glossy coat caught and reflected the sunlight, giving the animal an

almost glowing appearance. So bright was the shining red
of his mane that fire seemed to lick along the edges.

"It is the Fire-horse!"

The statement came as an awed gasp from one of the
young warriors. Then, as suddenly as he had appeared,
the stallion was gone, taking with him the fleeing mares
and foals.

Frantically, the last colt scrambled over the rimrock
and disappeared. Horse Seeker kneed his mount forward
to the top for one more glimpse.

There in the distance, the red stallion circled and gathered his band together, urging a lagging youngster, herd-
ing them toward the safety of the broken foothills. Horse
Seeker could only watch in mute admiration.

"It was the Fire-horse!"

Almost with reverence, the young warrior repeated his
statement to Horse Seeker.

"The Fire-horse?"

"Yes, Horse Seeker. He is a spirit-horse. Our people
have seen him before, but he can never be caught. He is
very dangerous."

Dangerous, yes, thought Horse Seeker. But a magnificent creature. A spirit-horse? Maybe. But for the man
whose medicine is strong enough to capture and control
him, what a victory! And what a race of horses such an
animal could sire!

That evening the stories at the fire were of horses.
Some were told and retold, mostly stories of the magical
spirit-animal, the Fire-horse, whose red mane burned like
the sun.

Horse Seeker had little to say, for once. He listened,
but his mind was racing ahead. There was so much
excitement in his head that he knew he would sleep
little.

He did not mention to his companions that he had
seen this animal before. That the Fire-horse of the River
People and the Dream-horse of his vision quest were one
and the same.

18

>> >> >>

As the hunting party traveled next day on the return journey to the camp of the River People, there was much excitement. Only one of the young men had ever seen the Fire-horse before, and then only at a distance. Here was an experience of a lifetime, one to be told and retold around the story fires for many seasons.

Each young rider recounted the experience repeatedly as they rode. Each retold where he had been when the great horse appeared on the rim of the basin.

Only Horse Seeker remained silent. The appearance of the stallion had affected him more profoundly than all the rest. It was a startling experience to suddenly discover that his Dream-horse was real, of flesh and blood. This answered one question that had long bothered him but raised another.

Now he knew of the Dream-horse, that it did exist, and where it might be found. Now he was faced with interpreting the meaning of these things. He was like a tracker following a trail in the sand, a trail made by a creature he has never seen. There was mystery and wonder and a hint of danger. Horse Seeker rode on, a little despondent.

The excitement of their experience was completely extinguished as they came near the camp. Black Otter, leader of the party, suddenly reined in his horse and held up a hand for silence.

From the valley ahead, a high-pitched wail could be heard, rising and falling on the wind.

"It is the Mourning Song! Someone is dead!"

The young warrior struck heels to his horse and loped ahead, followed by the rest.

Horse Seeker understood this perfectly. It would be the same with his own people. Families and friends were singing to mourn the unexpected loss.

The riders cantered into the camp, looking anxiously to see which families were bereaved. Two women knelt beside a fur-bundled corpse, wailing and tossing handfuls of dirt and ashes on their own heads and garments. One had gashed her forearms with some sharp instrument, and her hands were covered with dried and clotted blood.

From another quarter came more wailing. There must be more than one fatality. Almost frantic with worry now, Horse Seeker hurried toward the lodge of Spotted Elk. It was with great relief that he saw the door skin thrust aside and the slim figure of Yellow Bird come forward.

The girl ran to his horse, tragedy stark in her face.

"It is the Blue Paints! They have killed two of our young men."

The story was simple. Three of the youngest hunters of the band had encountered a party of Blue Paints while hunting. Walks-Like-Thunder had made a mockery of the youngsters, challenging them to fight, one at a time. Of course, it was no contest. He had brutally struck down two of the boys and then disarmed and released the third.

"This will show your River People the strength of the Blue Paints," he had admonished the youngster.

The boy had arrived back in camp on foot, angry, weeping, frustrated, and guilt-ridden for not having died with his friends.

"It was not your fault," the chief had assured.

There was no effort to mount a vengeance raid. It

would be foolish to do so against the superior strength of
the Blue Paints.

This had long been the pattern, Yellow Bird now explained to Horse Seeker. The brutish Walks-Like-Thunder
would encounter a chance warrior or two of her people
and go through the mockery of a challenge. Of course, it
was always a one-sided mismatch resulting in the death
of the other contestant.

In the past few seasons, the fighting strength of the
River People had been seriously reduced. There had been
some talk of returning to their previous existence as
growers in the river valleys. Meanwhile, conditions had
become worse and worse.

Now, for instance, there would be little hunting for a
time. It would be considered too dangerous to range far
from the camp, with Blue Paints in the area. Movement
would be restricted. If hunting was poor, there might yet
be a time of hunger.

As Yellow Bird sadly explained all these things, Horse
Seeker began to understand much more about these people and their problems. In the tragedy of the band over
their loss, his experience with the Dream-horse was almost forgotten. He had not even mentioned it to Yellow
Bird.

Horse Seeker had never considered himself a warrior or
decision maker. He had no aspirations to become a chief.
He was more content in the role of medicine man, following in the steps of his father. Yet now he found
himself studying the dilemma of Yellow Bird's people.

There must be a solution. As he evaluated the situation in his mind, the center of the problem seemed to
revolve around the one man, Walks-Like-Thunder. If he
could be defeated, his followers would lose their aggressive tendencies.

Horse Seeker sighed deeply. It began to look as if he
must meet the man in single combat. True, he had thrown
such a suggestion at the big man previously, but that had
been mostly talk. It was the bluster and bragging of long
tradition. Now it appeared that a direct challenge to the
power of the Blue Paint chief was the only way to free
the plains of his terrorism.

The young man could not have said why he felt it his
responsibility. He was not even among the most skilled

warriors of his people. Still, he had a deep personal mission, a sense of duty. He must personally recover the Spanish bit, the elk-dog medicine. Again, he felt the same dreamlike compulsion he had experienced earlier. Somehow he had become part of this series of events without having any choice in the matter. Things had been, and were, occurring which were affecting him, regardless of his own actions.

Yellow Bird accompanied him to care for his horse, and the two returned to the lodge. They had just arrived there when Pretty Basket hurried up.

"Horse Seeker!" she exclaimed, "I have heard that you have seen the Fire-horse!"

Her eyes danced with excitement.

Yellow Bird turned to him in astonishment.

"Really? The Fire-horse?"

Horse Seeker nodded abstractly. His mind was racing. He had seen no real connection between that experience and the problems of Yellow Bird's people, but now a pattern started to emerge.

Possibly, he realized, the oddly disconnected events of the past few moons had some meaning after all. The beginnings of a plan began to form in the misty recesses of his mind.

19
» »› ›»

"**H**orse Seeker, you have gone mad!"

The girl's large dark eyes seemed even larger with alarm.

"No, Yellow Bird. Someone must fight Walks-Like-Thunder and beat him. He is killing all the young warriors of your people, one at a time."

"But," she protested, "you will be killed too. You are brave, but he is a mighty warrior."

A tear glistened, and the girl's lower lip trembled a little.

Horse Seeker nodded.

"That is why there must be a special plan."

"But, Horse Seeker! To capture the Fire-horse? You may be killed even trying that!"

"No, little one," he smiled. "There are things I have not told you yet. I am a medicine man among my own people."

He saw no reason to specify that he was an apprentice medicine man, under his father's teaching.

"Do you remember the ornament around the neck of Walks-Like-Thunder?"

The girl nodded, still tearful.

"It is mine, the elk-dog medicine of my people. He stole it from me, and my mission is to recover it. That is why I must kill him."

"But the Fire-horse?"

"The horse is part of my medicine," he exaggerated a little. "He will help me to defeat Walks-Like-Thunder and restore the Elk-dog medicine to my tribe."

"But how, Horse Seeker?"

He paused a moment. There were many things he had not completely thought out yet.

"I will follow the Fire-horse and his herd until they think I am one of them. Then I will catch him and ask him to help me."

He wished that the whole scheme seemed as logical as he tried to make it sound. It had seemed reasonable when he thought of it in the quiet of darkness. It still must be the intended purpose of the Dream-horse. He could think of no other explanation.

Yellow Bird's face now glowed with admiration. It was encouraging to see that she believed in his ability to accomplish this thing.

"I will help you!" She offered eagerly.

"No, Yellow Bird. I will be traveling with the elk-dogs, becoming one of them, trying to get inside the head of their chief."

"But you must eat," she pleaded. "You cannot graze like the elk-dogs. I can bring you food."

It was reasonable, he had to admit. In following the herd, he would have no time to hunt and could carry few provisions. Yellow Bird could leave food at a prearranged place, and he could manage to return there every few days.

This brought forth another dilemma. How would Spotted Elk react to the idea of his daughter riding through the hills alone or with a young man of another tribe?

Horse Seeker had pondered this relationship at great length. The two young people had become so close that both assumed that they would eventually be married. It was such a certainty that it was not even necessary to discuss it.

Now, if they could proceed with marriage plans, Yellow Bird would be free to travel with her husband, to help him in any way needed. There could be no objection on the part of her father.

Yet, there were other obstacles to such a solution. Horse Seeker had nothing to give the girl's parents as a gift to help compensate them for their loss. Though he was well liked and respected among the girl's people, he had very little of material value. Even the weapons with which he hunted and the horses he rode were borrowed. He could not go empty-handed to the girl's father to ask for her. For now, he must postpone any such plans.

"Yellow Bird, let us tell everyone that I am leaving. I will borrow a horse, and you can ride a distance with me. Then we can make plans before you return."

So it was arranged. Horse Seeker was profuse in his thanks for the hospitality of the River People, especially to Spotted Elk and Bright Leaf. The latter, who had enjoyed having a handsome young warrior in the lodge, prepared a bundle of supplies for him to carry. She thanked him for hunting in behalf of the lodge of Spotted Elk during his stay.

Bright Leaf was a bit puzzled at the nonchalance with which the young people prepared to part. She had thought them much closer than this.

Spotted Elk remained a trifle suspicious. It was not in him to distrust his daughter. If she said she would ride a distance and return, she would do so. He remained uneasy, however. There was still much about this strange young man that had been left unsaid.

The two young people rode out and headed southeast, but as soon as they were out of sight they circled to the opposite direction. They must move rapidly so that Yellow Bird could return to camp before nightfall and avoid suspicion.

As they rode, Horse Seeker told of his general plan, and they selected a meeting place.

"Every three suns I will try to return there."

He pointed to an odd-shaped hill, topped by jumbled red boulders.

"If I am not there, leave the food. I will find it when I can."

They dismounted when they reached the hilltop.

"There, by the pine tree."

He indicated a hollow at the base of the tree, which would provide some protection from the weather.

Yellow Bird nodded absently, her thoughts elsewhere. This parting was more difficult than either had imagined.

"You will be careful, my warrior?"

Horse Seeker gathered the girl in his arms and held her closely against his chest. He could feel the flutter of her heartbeat, the soft warmth of her body. *Aiee*, this was not easy!

Finally he pushed her gently from him.

"You must go back, little one. Here, take my horse."

"No! Horse Seeker, you must not be on foot!"

"Yes, I must. The wild elk-dogs will not let me come near them if I am mounted. Now, go!"

He assisted her to her horse's back and handed her the rein of the other animal.

"Tell your father I was preparing to catch an elk-dog to ride."

Both smiled at the little joke, but a bit sadly.

"It will go well, Yellow Bird. My medicine is strong."

She nodded, not really convinced. She could see many problems and wished that she had more confidence in Horse Seeker's plan.

But now she must leave quickly to be back at her parents' lodge by dark. Reluctantly, she turned her mare and touched a heel to the flank.

"Yellow Bird!" Horse Seeker called after her.

"Yes?" The girl turned eagerly.

"Yellow Bird, there is one more thing I have not told you."

She sat, afraid of what she might hear as they parted. Horse Seeker saw her dismay and realized that he had frightened her.

"No, no, it is nothing bad," he assured her.

Now the whole thing was becoming embarrassing. She probably thought he had failed to tell her about his wife and family among his own people.

"It is only about my name," he blurted. "I am not called Horse Seeker. I made it up. My name is Rabbit."

His face broke into a broad, embarrassed grin, and his prominent front teeth shone white in the afternoon sunlight. Yellow Bird chuckled softly, the lilting sound that always reminded him of the ripple of water over stones.

"But now," she reminded him with her gentle smile, "you *are* Horse Seeker."

20

>> >> >>

Horse Seeker sat on a boulder, chewing strips of his dried meat supply while the girl watched from a few paces away.

It had taken him five suns to feel that he was making any progress. Only now, many days later, was he beginning to see a pattern in the movements of the animals.

His plan had been simple. He would find the herd of the Dream-horse and follow it. The medicine men of the People had followed buffalo in this way for many lifetimes.

At first, the animals ran wildly at his approach. He would wait until they stopped and then approach again. In a few days the horses began to accept him. Their acceptance was very tentative, involving a degree of mistrust. It was much like the attitude of a buffalo herd toward the wolves that circle its edges. The scavengers are recognized as a potential hazard, but not immediate enough to warrant alarm.

Thus the mare band of the Dream-horse slowly came to accept the presence of young Horse Seeker. It was painfully slow. Sometimes he would be near the peacefully grazing animals, apparently accepted. Then suddenly a stray puff of wind would startle a young mare with its telltale scent of man. The entire band would jump and run, and Horse Seeker would plod doggedly after them.

All the while he was attempting to become closer to them in spirit. He must not only move when the horses did, and drink with them, but he must get inside their heads, think with them, become one with them, until he was part of the herd. He must even smell like one of their number.

So, gradually, over many days and nights, he was accepted as part of the herd. If not part of it, at least a companion. He could walk freely among them and could even touch some of the more trusting individuals.

One black mare soon allowed him to place his hands freely on her body. Her shaggy winter hair was shedding by handfuls, and Horse Seeker discovered white marks on her withers and back.

"*Aiee*, mother, you have worn a saddle," he crooned softly, in surprise.

He saw little of the Dream-horse. The great red stallion made his presence known nearly every day, but usually at a distance. The animal was uncanny in his ability to use light and shadow to his advantage. Repeatedly, when the horse was close enough for Horse Seeker to have seen him well, it was impossible. Sunlight behind the animal prevented any but a poorly seen silhouette.

Once he saw the stallion in action by moonlight. A curious foal had wandered too far from its mother. Horse Seeker, watching, had just noticed the youngster when he saw a sinuous movement among the rocks on the hillside.

The cougar moved so smoothly that it seemed to flow toward the foal. The young man stared, entranced by the scene. He might have shouted, but the sound would not come. He told himself later that he had kept silent to avoid spoiling all his efforts to become one of the herd, but it was not true. He had been spellbound by the smooth efficiency of the real-cat.

The animal stopped now and crouched frozen for the space of a few heartbeats. It seemed to disappear in the light and shadow of moonlight on the hillside. Horse Seeker thought for a moment that it had been only a

spirit. Then the great cat charged, a deadly rash at the
unsuspecting foal.

The colt screamed in terror and bolted just as the
real-cat struck. It was a glancing blow, only partially
effective. The foal rolled and struggled to its feet to run.
Its anxious mother hurried forward, calling to her terrified colt, terrified herself, but ready to protect her young.
The cougar wheeled for another rush.

Then, out of nowhere came the Dream-horse. One
moment he was not there, and suddenly he was. The cat
crouched, snarling, undecided whether to fight or run. It
was plain to Horse Seeker that the cat saw a great difference between attacking one small elk-dog and facing an
angry stallion.

The Dream-horse reared high in the air, striking at the
cougar with flashing hooves. The cat retreated, pursued
only a short distance by the stallion. Then all was quiet
again. The foal ran to his mother and began to nurse
while she nuzzled him comfortingly.

The stallion, still snorting and tossing his head, suddenly stopped to look directly at Horse Seeker. The young
man sat very still but prepared to run for his life if
necessary. He was in the open, some distance from any
protection, and the stallion still raged in anger.

Then the Dream-horse apparently recognized his crouch-
ing figure as the constant companion of recent days.
With one final snort, the horse drifted off to graze. Horse
Seeker breathed a long sigh of relief.

From that time, even the red Dream-horse seemed to
accept his presence. The animal eyed him with suspicion, but as long as he did not try to approach too closely,
he was tolerated.

Now, he could begin to see some pattern in the movements of the Dream-horse's band. He saw that they remained in a long oval-shaped territory lying north and
south against the foothills. Unless they were disturbed,
their movements were quite predictable. Every three or
four suns found the herd at the same places.

There were three watering places in the area. Two
were clear, cold streams and the third a spring which
trickled out of the rock at the head of a narrow canyon.
The canyon had steep walls, and some of the more flighty
of the horses seemed to dislike this watering place. Horse

Seeker could understand this. His own preferences were for more open country with distant horizons. But water had to be taken where it could be found. This was the only source at the south end of the herd's territory.

It was this fact that led to the formation of a specific plan. Horse Seeker had long since given up the idea of trying to rope the red stallion in the open. There was no way that one man with a rope could hope to hold the great horse.

But here, in the canyon, it would be different. He rose to walk up and down the canyon, pacing distances, examining with special care a narrow portion of the gorge where brush and trees grew thickly. He grunted to himself in satisfaction and set off at a trot for his meeting place with Yellow Bird.

The girl was waiting when he arrived, seated on one of the red boulders. This part was most difficult of all. She must not touch him, must not even be upwind from him, lest some stray scent cling to his body and alarm his quarry. They stood several paces apart, smiling, longing to hold each other but unable to do so.

At least they could see each other. For a time, before the patterns of the herd's movements had been recognized, they had missed meeting several times. Yellow Bird had brought food, waited, and had to leave in disappointment. Now, the routine had been established, and they could look forward to meeting.

The girl spoke first.

"How is it with you?"

"Good," he nodded, "and I have a plan."

Excitedly, he outlined the scheme.

"I will need a small axe," he finished, "and another rope. I will have to use this one for lashings."

He indicated the coil around his shoulder.

"Yes, but you must eat now."

She pointed to the bundle on a nearby rock and seated herself again. Horse Seeker opened the pack and began to chew.

"Will you come tomorrow?"

"So soon? Will the herd be back then?"

"No, but I will stay here and start work at the canyon. I will finish before the elk-dogs return."

The girl nodded, glanced at the lowering sun, and walked to her spotted mare.

"Be careful, Horse Seeker. I will see you tomorrow."

21

>> >> >>

By the time Yellow Bird returned the following day, much of the work was done. Horse Seeker had cut off the knotted end of his rawhide rope and unraveled it, carefully saving each piece of the thongs from which it was plaited.

He gathered such brush and down timber as he was able, with no tools except his knife. Some he could break loose or pry apart to drag to the selected area. There, at the narrow neck of the canyon, he began to construct a barricade.

Already, the barrier had been partly formed by nature. Rock slides had tumbled a clutter of boulders among the trees, partially blocking the way. The trail swung wide to the left to avoid the foot of the slide. Horse Seeker carried stones until his back ached, piling the scattered blocks to make the slide even more impassable. Yet, it must not be an obvious change in appearance.

When he tired of carrying and lifting rocks, he turned again to building the brush barricade. It was much like the winter windbreaks used by the People to shelter their lodges, but higher and stronger. Stout poles and heavy brush were lashed firmly against the up-canyon side of the trees with the thongs from his rope. These lashings would only carry the already familiar scent to which the horses had become accustomed.

Wherever he could, Horse Seeker used existing brush and trees to hide his barricade. From time to time he would walk a few paces away and turn to look at the growing barrier. It must be high enough to prevent jumping and strong enough to keep the animals from attempting to push through.

In all his comings and goings, Horse Seeker was careful to avoid the path. It must show no telltale sign to the suspicious senses of the Dream-horse.

At the proper place, the trail passed between two trees, only two or three paces apart. There he would construct his doorway. It would be of stout poles, to be cut when Yellow Bird returned with an axe. He had already selected the slim trees he needed in a stand of pine some distance away. He would cut them to size there and carry them to the canyon. In that way, no scatter of fresh chips would leave telltale sign and scent.

He was fortunate in one respect. Near the entrance to the canyon, but some distance from his barrier, a porcupine spent the night chewing in the top of a pine tree near the trail. The completely natural appearance and scent of pine cuttings would lull the suspicions of the elk-dogs, distracting them from the changed appearance of the trail ahead.

Yellow Bird arrived at the appointed time, carrying a new rawhide rope and her father's stone axe.

"My father is becoming suspicious, Horse Seeker. He does not wish me to ride alone."

"I know, little one. It will not be much longer. If you must, tell Spotted Elk what we are doing."

She shook her head.

"Not yet. After you catch your Dream-horse, maybe."

Horse Seeker nodded.

"It is good. Put the rope in that tree. I will not touch it yet. The smell might cling to me."

She left the axe on a boulder. It would not carry so new a scent. In any case, he must handle it immediately to finish his barrier.

"I wish I could show you, Yellow Bird. The trap goes well."

"No matter. I will see it with the Dream-horse inside," she smiled.

Again, Horse Seeker longed to hold her in his arms. This entire plan could not have been accomplished without her.

"When shall I come again?"

"Three suns," he counted. "The herd will be back in two, and we may have caught the Dream-horse."

Yellow Bird swung to the back of her spotted mare and waved to him.

"I am eager to see him."

Horse Seeker lost no time in picking up the axe. He hurried to the pines to continue his plan. Several trips were required to carry the assortment of poles and limbs for the completion of the barrier.

It was one full day after he finished the trap before the horse herd would be expected. Impatient, he adjusted and readjusted poles and brush repeatedly. Finally, he realized that he could only leave more scent to cause suspicion and left the area.

He climbed to the top of a nearby rock, spread his robe, and stretched out in the warm sunlight. He had intended only to rest, but soon he slept, tired from his exertions. There were strange, fragmented dreams, of Blue Paints, elk-dogs, the Dream-horse, and, above all, the smiling face of Yellow Bird. The girl had become so much a part of his life. Horse Seeker reveled in her smile, her bright, quick insight, and her understanding.

His half-formed dream was shattered by a raucous sound, the coarse calling of a crow. Startled, he sat up. The bird was perched in a gnarled pine that clung to a crack in the rock hardly an arm's length from where he lay. Confused and sleepy, he stared dully. The crow stared back for a moment, then rose into the air, circled, and flew away.

Puzzled, Horse Seeker watched it go. Was there some meaning here?

Something moved to the north, in his range of vision but beyond the slowly flying crow. Quickly he sat up, straining to see. Several plumes of dust rose from different points along the dry, level plain. It took only a moment to understand the situation.

The horses were returning.

Horse Seeker sprang to his feet and raced for the canyon. He must be hidden before the red stallion entered the doorway. Then he could drop the heavy door of poles into place, closing off all escape.

Panting from exertion, he sprinted along the trail and dodged behind the barricade just as the first mares and foals began to move into sight at the canyon's mouth. The animals slowed to a walk, wanting to move on to drink but cautious from long experience.

A hundred paces away, the leading mare stopped to snort in alarm at the porcupine tree with its scent of fresh pine resin. The black mare with saddle scars pushed past, hardly pausing when she entered the trap. The others followed, the foals finally breaking into a run for the spring basin.

Then the young man saw the Dream-horse. The animal moved so smoothly, so quietly, yet showed such magnificent strength. Muscles rippled as the horse tiptoed along the trail. Horse Seeker's hand tightened on the pole which would close the opening when he shoved, and he held his breath. Truly, this must be the chief of all elk-dogs.

The stallion was suspicious. He paused only a moment at the gnawed pine, then seemed to decide that this was no threat. He slowed to a nervous, dancing walk, peering ahead. Plainly, the leading mares had encountered no danger, but the stallion seemed unsure.

The head of the Dream-horse was actually inside the trap when something startled him. Horse Seeker was never certain of the cause. Perhaps an unfamiliar smell or the unnatural droop of a wilting leaf in the brush barricade. It was no matter, now.

The stallion dropped his hindquarters and pivoted, the great driving muscles of his thighs straining as they bunched to thrust forward. The animal called out as he whirled the alarm call to his mare band, the unforgettable scream that is both warning and challenge.

In the space of a heartbeat, the mare band was in motion, running frantically for the opening. For a moment, Horse Seeker was tempted to close the pole door, but he resisted the impulse. He would have the red Dream-horse or none.

Choking in the dust of their passing, Horse Seeker sat dejected while the last frightened foal scampered to safety. The many days of heat, cold, thirst, and exhaustion were of no use. The hard work of the past three suns was as nothing.

He had failed again.

22

>> >> >>

Yellow Bird was expected at the meeting place the following day. Horse Seeker waited for her with a heavy heart. He would have to tell her of his failure.

Even worse, he had no better plan. It might take some time to win again the confidence of the red stallion's band. They had been threatened once by association with the strange creature who walked on two legs. Now they would be even more wary.

He must try again. He could have followed the herd immediately. Perhaps he should have, but he felt that the girl deserved to know the situation. If she returned and found no sign of him now, she would be concerned. When they had parted, their plan had seemed to be working. If Horse Seeker failed to keep their meeting, she would think the worst, imagining him dead or injured. She might even come looking for him, and that could be disastrous. If his carefully built trap became contaminated with the scent of the girl and the horse she rode, the animals might never enter the canyon again.

It was growing late, and Yellow Bird should have been here by now. Horse Seeker was worried. Could it be that

she had encountered the Blue Paints? He paced and fret-
ted, straining to see into the distance.

Finally he saw her. It seemed an eternity that he watched
the approach of the spotted mare. Yellow Bird sat arrow-
straight, hands firm on the reins. He could tell even at a
distance that she was angry.

Without a word, she rode up, swung a slim leg over the
animal's withers, and jumped lightly to the ground. Her
face was still dark with rage.

Once more, he resisted the temptation to take her in
his arms.

"There is something wrong?"

"No, no, only this useless mare."

"What is the matter?"

"It is nothing, Horse Seeker. The mare is excited and
hard to manage. She is in season."

Of course, he thought. A mare in season is unpredict-
able, unmanageable. Her head is filled with thoughts of
romance and not with sensibility. He could sympathize
with the difficulty that the girl might have encountered
on her journey from the camp. Even now, the mare
pranced nervously, head high. Her ears pricked forward,
and her eyes roved over the far distances, seeking companions. She nickered, long and loud, calling to any elk-
dogs within earshot. There was no doubt. A mare in
season could be a dreadful nuisance.

Then another thought struck him. Perhaps this situation could be used to his advantage. A horse, like a
human with romance on his mind, thinks of little else.
Certainly not of dangers like traps and barricades.

"Yellow Bird! I know how to catch the Dream-horse!"

"You did not catch him?"

"Not yet."

He was excited now, bubbling with enthusiasm as he
outlined a new plan.

"Of course, I need your mare," he finished.

"Yes, yes, Horse Seeker."

His enthusiasm was readily transmitted. Excitedly they
discussed the plan.

"But what about you?" Horse Seeker asked. "Your
family will expect you back."

There was a long discussion. What was practical, what
was desirable, what was even possible were discussed.

Yellow Bird wished to stay with him, but there were
many things against it. Aside from worry to her people,
they could not camp near the trap in the canyon. Horse
Seeker must stay at the trap, which again would leave
the girl alone. In addition, they must still avoid contact
because of the risk of transferring the girl's scent and
alarming the horses. It would be risky enough to have
the mare with her unfamiliar smell in the canyon.

It was finally decided. The two would return to the
village as rapidly as possible, and Horse Seeker would
return with the mare. He could only hope that the animal would remain in her present condition until the
stallion returned. He inquired about this as they set off,
the girl riding and Horse Seeker jogging alongside.

"When did the mare come in?"

"Yesterday."

"It is good. She should still be ready when the Dream-
horse returns."

He had estimated quickly. A vigorous young mare
should be receptive from three to five suns. With any
favorable medicine at all, she should be at her peak of
desire when the herd returned. He tried to ignore the
possibility that the alarm of their last visit might cause
the elk-dogs to change their territory.

The young couple reached an area near the camp before darkness fell. Horse Seeker had already reminded the
girl that he could not go closer because of the myriad
smells of the village.

"You really do think like an elk-dog," she chided.

She swung down and handed him the rein.

"May it go well with you, Horse Seeker."

"Yellow Bird," he began hesitantly, "will you come
again in three suns?"

"Of course."

"It is good."

He hesitated again. There was so much that he wished
to say.

"You should tell your father now what is happening."

"Yes," she giggled, "he will wonder how I lost a
horse."

"But tell no one else."

The girl nodded.

"Yes, Horse Seeker. Now, go."

He sprang to the back of the spotted mare and turned quickly away. Somehow this parting was more difficult than all the others. The animal called out loudly at being forced to leave familiar surroundings and companions again. Another horse answered from somewhere

Horse Seeker could sympathize. He cast one backward glance toward the village. Yellow Bird was walking straightaway toward the lodges, tall and slim among the lengthening shadows of evening. She did not look back.

He turned away again and touched heels to the flanks of the spotted mare. There was much to do, back at the canyon, and all must be ready before the return of the Dream-horse.

23

» » »

Spotted Elk stood before his lodge among the length-ening shadows and watched his daughter stride across the meadow. She was on foot. He shook his head despair-ingly. She had been riding her spotted mare when she departed. How had she lost her horse?

Something was going on which Spotted Elk did not understand. The girl was behaving very strangely, had been ever since the departure of the young stranger, Horse Seeker. Her father was puzzled. He had talked to her friend, Pretty Basket, who knew nothing. In fact Pretty Basket, too, was somewhat irritated by Yellow Bird's secretive behavior.

Spotted Elk had become increasingly concerned by his daughter's unexplained absences. True, there had been no enemies in the area for some time now. Still, it was dangerous for anyone to leave the camp alone, especially for most of a day at a time. This daughter of his was a real problem, a headstrong, firm-willed woman.

Now, somehow, she had lost her spotted mare. It was time to have a discussion.

The girl approached with a smile and a wave. She

should have been upset, tired, unhappy over the loss of
her horse. Instead, she seemed cheerful and energetic.
Spotted Elk rankled, irritated. This self-willed daughter
of his must be taught proper behavior.

He took a few steps forward and started to speak sternly
to her, but the girl interrupted.

"Father, I must talk with you."

She took his hand and pulled him gently toward the
bend of the stream, a favorite place of hers for solitary
meditation.

Spotted Elk followed, confused. Could it be that he
was to be informed as to what was happening? Again he
thought, how frustrating to raise a daughter like this one.
He had been ready to demand a conversation, and now
she had initiated it. He sighed inwardly. How can one
criticize a person who already agrees to one's wishes?

The girl sat on the smooth bole of a fallen cottonwood
tree and indicated a place beside her. Spotted Elk sat.

"Father, there is much to tell."

He nodded, waiting.

Yellow Bird poured forth her story and the unanswered
facts about the stranger, Horse Seeker. Spotted Elk's head
whirled in confusion. The young man's mission, his status as a medicine man, his ambition to defeat the dreaded
Walks-Like-Thunder.

"You mean, Horse Seeker is still here? He did not
return to his people?"

"No, no, Father. He is capturing the Fire-horse."

"But what has the Fire-horse to do with this?"

"Horse Seeker saw this chief of horses in a dream.
That is why he is called Horse Seeker. He calls this the
Dream-horse."

"But what has this to do with the Blue Paints?"

"Horse Seeker must fight Walks-Like-Thunder and kill
him to recover the elk-dog medicine of his people."

"He will be killed!"

The girl paused for only a moment of doubt.

"No!" she stated firmly. "He will not! The Dream-
horse will help him strike down Walks-Like-Thunder!"

"Ah, daughter, I do not know. Is the medicine of Horse
Seeker this strong?"

Again the girl's lip trembled a bit as she paused. Then
her confidence returned.

"Yes, Father. If he can catch his Dream-horse, it proves the strength of his medicine."

Spotted Elk was not convinced.

"But how will he do this?"

"That," she smiled, "is why I returned on foot."

She described the plan of Horse Seeker, becoming more excited as she talked. Spotted Elk nodded.

It was possible, he began to see, that he had completely underestimated the young man. Yes, the plan might work. He had to admire the manner in which Horse Seeker intended to use the powerful medicine of the young mare to assist his own.

Still, there was much danger ahead. The capture of the great red stallion would be only the first step. If Horse Seeker's medicine proved strong enough to catch and then to tame the animal, the hardest part still remained. Spotted Elk was respected as a hunter and warrior. Yet, he himself would feel inadequate to attempt hand-to-hand combat with the fearsome chief of the Blue Paints.

Ah well, one thing at a time. First, it must be seen whether Horse Seeker would succeed in capturing his Dream-horse. There were still some questions in the mind of Spotted Elk.

"And you have been riding out to see this Horse Seeker?"

"Yes, Father. I have been taking food."

An idea began to grow in the mind of Spotted Elk.

"When do you go again?"

"Three suns. The elk-dogs return each three or four days."

He nodded.

"I will go with you."

He had half expected the girl to refuse, but she thought only a moment.

"It is good, Father. Horse Seeker wished me to tell you of his plans. But we must tell no one else. If people go out to see what is happening, it might destroy everything."

"Yes. No one, except your mother. She has been worried, too."

Yellow Bird nodded.

"But no one else!"

"It is good. Now, let us go and talk to your mother. We must find ways to help Horse Seeker."

Bright Leaf watched from in front of her lodge as the two approached from the direction of the stream. Even at a distance she could see a change in her daughter's manner. Yellow Bird bounced along with a spring in her step, chattering like a magpie to her father.

Bright Leaf smiled to herself. At last there was some sign that the girl was beginning to come out of her secretive mood. Her mother had been as concerned as Spotted Elk, but they had talked little of it. There was nothing to talk of. It had been more of a feeling, a vague lack of communication. Bright Leaf had been aware that the girl was taking food somewhere. But for what purpose? She suspected that it had to do with Horse Seeker, but why would the young man still be in the area after a very uneventful departure?

Ah well, the girl would tell them when the time was right. Meanwhile, it was to be hoped that her activities were not too dangerous.

Now, as Yellow Bird and her father approached the lodge, the girl ran ahead, her eyes glistening with excitement.

"Mother! We have much to tell you!"

24

» » »

It was fully dark when Horse Seeker reined the spotted mare to a stop at the entrance to the canyon. He slid from the animal's back and led her forward a few steps. The mare peered into the darkness of strange surroundings, head up and ears pricked forward.

Nervously she called, seeking others of her kind, but there was no answer. Still excited, she nickered again. Horse Seeker stood anxiously watching in the dim starlight. Could it be too late already?

The mare danced around him in a circle at the end of the rawhide rein, then stopped to raise her tail and urinate.

Horse Seeker smiled and sighed with relief. This was what he had planned. The spot was now marked with the powerful medicine of an excited young mare. It would be irresistible to the senses of any stallion coming near.

He led the mare a few steps nearer the trap, still a bow shot away, then stopped again. The animal quieted somewhat, nibbled at a tuft of new grass, and finally repeated her ritual.

Three times more, Horse Seeker patiently waited for the repetition of the mare's medicine ceremony. Each

time they had progressed only a few paces before stopping again, but now they were actually nearing the opening in the barrier. He glanced at the eastern sky, knowing
the dawn was near.

When Horse Seeker felt they were close enough, he led
the mare rapidly through the gap in the barrier. He wanted
no possibility that the stallion would pause in the opening long enough to investigate. A few paces inside, then
one more stop to mark the way.

He led the mare to water, then back to within plain
sight of the doorway. Here he tied her firmly and went to
gather some grass and tender young cottonwood browse
to keep her occupied.

There was now nothing but to wait. The anxious
thought crossed his mind that after the previous alarm
the Dream-horse might leave the area entirely and not
return here at all. He tried to put such thoughts from his
mind.

It was growing light now, the creatures of the night
seeking their lodges while the awakening day creatures
began to stir and voice greetings to the coming of Sun
Boy. A crow swooped low over the canyon and uttered
three shrill cries. Horse Seeker was never certain whether
this was the medicine crow or not, but it was reassuring.

That day and much of the next were very slow and
boring. He rested, ate, and took the mare to water again.
He was pleased to note that the animal appeared still to
be strongly in season. He wandered idly around the area,
in a way thankful for a day with no demands.

It was not until the following afternoon that things
began to occur. His first sign came in the form of a cry
from the spotted mare. She had been calling from time to
time, but there was something different about this. It
was more specific, more definite.

Horse Seeker sprang up and hurried to a vantage point
from which to see the land. Yes, there in the distance,
across the flat, came the plumes of dust as before. The
band of the Dream-horse had returned. The young man
sprinted back to the canyon to his hiding place behind
the barrier.

It was still sometime before the animals approached.
Their demeanor was calm, unexcited. Good, Horse Seeker
told himself. They had decided that the area was still safe.

Once again, the first colts plunged blindly ahead, the more cautious animals moving more slowly and carefully. The spotted mare was calling frantically to the approaching herd. The newcomers first stopped, staring curiously, then moved forward to investigate.

Horse Seeker was so engrossed in watching the greeting ceremony between the wild horses and the stranger that he almost failed to notice the Dream-horse.

The red stallion had stopped to sniff at the first medicine place left by the mare. His movements were now ritualistic, patterned like a dance. Horse Seeker watched, entranced.

The stallion slowly extended his neck, pointing his nose at the sky. His upper lip curled up and back, exposing front teeth. The ears flattened against the neck of the creature, seeming to become invisible as the horse slowly swung his head back and forth with a serpentine motion.

Then the trance was somehow broken, and the Dream-horse trotted forward. Only once more did he pause for an abbreviated repeat of his dance.

Suddenly the spotted mare squealed. There was an instant grunting answer from the stallion as he shouldered forward. It appeared to Horse Seeker that the Dream-horse did not even notice the barrier as he trotted through the opening.

There was another exchange of squeals, and the stallion arched his neck forward to bite the mare playfully on the withers. She squealed again and swung her hips toward him, launching a kick that was mostly pretense. The Dream-horse rose to his full height on muscular hind legs, arching his body across that of the waiting mare.

Horse Seeker was so preoccupied that he nearly forgot his principal purpose. Recovering suddenly, he gave a heave on the pole that balanced the gate. The heavy structure began to move, swinging downward to crash in place between the trees. The canyon was closed. The Dream-horse was his.

For a moment, Horse Seeker thought that there would be no reaction at all. Then the stallion seemed to realize that he had been duped. The horse whirled to charge directly at the barrier. For a moment, it seemed that he would attempt the jump. Then he wheeled away. Horse

Seeker nodded to himself, pleased. The red stallion had good judgment. Even in the excitement and stress of the moment, the horse had decided against an impossible attempt, one which may have resulted in injury.

The mares and foals milled about uncertainly, some moving on into the canyon to water, some standing confused.

Two more attempts to escape, the stallion tried. Once he attempted to climb the rock slide and once to breach the wall of brush, both unsuccessfully. Then he returned to stand at the pole gate, which closed the opening to freedom. For the first time he seemed to notice the figure of Horse Seeker, still half hidden near the opening.

For a moment, the young man made ready to run for his life if the stallion attacked. Then slowly he rose and stepped into the open. The two, man and horse, looked long into each other's eyes. Then the stallion whirled away to run to the other end of the canyon.

Horse Seeker watched in admiration.

"It is good, Dream-horse," he muttered after the stallion. "We shall yet be friends."

25
>> >> >>

Horse Seeker soon realized that he had created a problem. Penned in the canyon were some twenty mares, with nearly as many foals, in addition to the Dream-horse, which had been the major goal. It required little thought to realize that in a very short while the grass and other scant browse in the canyon would be exhausted.

Much as he regretted the need, he must release the other horses. *Aiee*, many times he had dreamed of being able to own such a herd of elk-dogs. And these, fleet and strong, the foals carrying the blood of the Dream-horse! The People would hardly believe such good fortune. But the thing was beyond his control. He could not endanger his primary mission, even with the effort to save these fine mares and foals.

But for now, they could be of use. Before he could even remove the barrier to release them, it would be necessary to rope the red stallion and have him partly restrained.

Horse Seeker uncoiled his rope and shook out the stiffness, then untied the spotted mare and swung to her back. Slowly, he began to walk the mare through and around the milling animals, talking and singing in a soft, crooning voice.

At first the elk-dogs fled wildly at his approach, but soon they did no more than move aside as he passed. The black mare with saddle marks was among the first to calm.

Before dark, he had calmed the band to the extent that he could lay hands on several of the animals. At no time, however, had he been able to approach the stallion. The Dream-horse did not retreat in terror; he simply moved out of the way. There was seldom a moment when the clear eye of the stallion failed to watch each movement of his captor.

With the coming of darkness, Horse Seeker dismounted and released the mare to mingle with the others. He waved to the stallion as he climbed out of the trap.

That night, for the first in a long while, Horse Seeker was able to sit by a fire and sleep curled next to its warmth. Somehow this became a very important thing. He was warmed not only in his body but in spirit, and it seemed that his medicine was good.

At daylight he was again among the horses. They were calmer now, and he walked among them talking softly. The black mare was completely unafraid, and he selected her for his use today.

Carefully he worked, around and around, at a slow walk. He rode through, between, among, every varied pattern possible, calming the horses as they became accustomed to one of their number with a rider.

Before Sun Boy reached the top of his run, Horse Seeker found that he could gather and herd the mare band, keeping them closely bunched. An idea began to form in his mind. He had already decided that it might be possible to keep one or two of the calmer mares, sending them back with Yellow Bird. The black mare with saddle marks, especially, he had found to be well trained and useful.

Now he began to think in terms of keeping most of the animals. Yellow Bird would return on the following day, and with her help it might easily be possible to herd the entire band.

Meanwhile, such an attempt would depend entirely on his ability to catch the red stallion. Even in the confines

of the canyon, this showed possibilities of becoming quite
a task. The horse seemed always at the opposite end of
the enclosure, watchful, suspicious.

After innumerable attempts to approach on horseback,
Horse Seeker abandoned that plan. He stepped down and
released the black mare. For the rest of the day, he
moved on foot, slowly and quietly. He did not even
uncoil his rope but wore it around his shoulder.

The task seemed endless, and at times Horse Seeker
almost despaired at the plan he had undertaken. Gradually, however, the horse became more trusting. His
movements were calmer, more nonchalant. Horse Seeker
uncoiled his rope.

The sight of the dangling loops seemed to alarm the
stallion again, and it required more steps up and down
the canyon to regain his confidence.

Horse Seeker noticed that at one point in the stallion's
retreat the animal always took the same path. It was at
the rocky end of the slope, and each time the horse
escaped his approach by slipping between two huge rocks,
taller than a man. This maneuver put one of the rocks
between the horse and his pursuer, allowing escape to
the other end once more.

Horse Seeker studied the spot carefully from all angles.
He climbed to the top of one of the rocks to look down
on the passage between. A few scrubby bushes clung
precariously in cracks in the stone, and one small pine
grew almost directly in the narrow pathway. Overhead, a
branch of a large pine arched across the opening. Horse
Seeker almost laughed aloud in his satisfaction.

Quietly, he arranged his rope. When the end was tied
firmly to the limb overhead, he lowered the rest of the
coil to the ground below. He descended, walked around
the rock, and spread the loop around the opening. It was
easily held in place by draping it across or along the
scrubby bushes. The lower portion of the loop was kept
waist-high and partially concealed by means of the small
pine. The stallion had repeatedly brushed past the small
tree without harm. In addition, the young man knew
that a horse does not see well directly ahead. There
would be a space of a few heartbeats within the narrow
passage when the stallion would not see the danger. That
would be all the time needed.

He turned, still moving slowly, and walked among the
horses toward the Dream-horse. Now would be the most
critical part of the plan. He dreaded that some other
animal might accidently run into the loop. Then there
would be very little possibility that the red stallion could
be induced to go through the narrow path again.

Carefully he circled, singing softly. The stallion moved
aside, stepped lightly around Horse Seeker, and trotted
briskly to the other end of the enclosure. The young man
pursued, slowly but relentlessly, walking and singing his
soothing song of elk-dog medicine. The Dream-horse
moved away as he had numerous times before, glancing
back at the pursuer.

The two approached the place where the stallion had
repeatedly turned, and the animal did so again. He stepped
daintily around the rock, ducked his head, and lunged
through the narrow passage. The noose tightened as the
Dream-horse realized the danger and began to fight the
restraint.

Horse Seeker sprang to the top of the rock, his knife
ready to cut the rope if necessary to avoid injury to the
animal. The great horse screamed, reared high in the air,
and struck out with his forefeet.

Two rushes he made. The first was the lunge through
the narrow passage, ending with the abrupt choking stop
as the rope tightened. After a moment of confused fighting, the horse scrambled back through the opening, only
to hit the rope's end once more. The tree shuddered as
the great horse's weight smashed against the taut rope.

Horse Seeker was elated. The rope and the tree branch
had held both times without breaking. Even better, it
was apparent that the Dream-horse was highly intelligent. He did not attempt another dash, which would
have ended in a choking smash at the rope's end. He
danced, fought, snorted, and struck, but it seemed no
longer that he might injure himself.

At last the Dream-horse stood quietly, chest heaving,
streaked with sweat, trembling with exhaustion. Atop
the rock, Horse Seeker was also sweating and trembling.
He was exhausted from the day's excitement. He sat
down and called to the stallion below, gently and softly.

"You see, Dream-horse, I will not harm you."

The stallion cocked his head to one side to stare upward at his captor. There was no fear or even anger in the gaze, only curiosity.

Horse Seeker sat and sang softly until Sun Boy disappeared to go to his lodge behind the mountains. Finally he rose and descended to the ground.

"Tomorrow," he promised. "Tomorrow, my friend!"

26

» » »

Twice during the night, Horse Seeker rose to go and see that the horse was safe. The animal had found that it was possible to move back and forth between the rocks a few paces. Beyond that, the rope drew uncomfortably tight.

At each visit, Horse Seeker sat for a short while, talking and singing softly. Each time, the horse became nervous and excited at his approach but calmed as the young man sang.

On his visit at daylight, Horse Seeker brought an armful of freshly gathered grass. Very cautiously, he approached the stallion. To place the food where the horse could reach it, it would be necessary to place himself within striking distance of the deadly hooves.

He watched the animal closely, ready to drop the grass and dodge to safety, but there seemed no need. The Dream-horse retreated to the opposite end of his restraint, alert and watchful. There was one moment when the animal's ears flattened, and Horse Seeker nearly turned to run. Then the threat passed, and the young man carefully laid his armful of grass on the ground.

"Come and eat, my brother," he crooned softly.

It was apparent that the horse wished to do so but was distrustful.

"Come, we have food. I mean you no harm."

Still, it was not until Horse Seeker moved back that the stallion stepped daintily forward. The nostrils dilated, and the large dark eyes sought any hint of danger as the animal moved between the rocks. Repeatedly, he sniffed and snorted, and at last he nibbled a mouthful of the dewy-fresh grass.

"You see," Horse Seeker crooned softly, "there is no harm."

He sat, near but beyond arm's reach, while the stallion ate. Then he rose, moved slowly away, and returned with more food. This time the stallion came forward with less hesitancy.

It would still be necessary to allow the horse to water. Horse Seeker climbed the rock again and placed a hand on the rope below the limb. The stallion pulled back in alarm, but only briefly. Encouraged, Horse Seeker pulled gently on the nearly taut rope. The horse stepped forward to relieve the pull, and he relaxed the tension.

For some time the game continued. Soon he could induce the animal to step forward, stop, and resume walking. Eventually, the Dream-horse would walk through the passage, turn, and go back the other way, all by signals conveyed by the rope above.

Horse Seeker was becoming excited at the prospects now. This Dream-horse proved as intelligent as he was beautiful. The young man glanced at the sky. It would not be long until Yellow Bird arrived at the meeting place.

With great caution, he untied the rope from the overhead limb. Keeping it fairly taut, he now maneuvered the horse back and forth through the passage, holding the rope only with his hands.

The animal's reaction at this time would be all-important. If the Dream-horse panicked, or if he made a run to escape, there was no way Horse Seeker could hold him.

The young man's palms were sweaty as he quietly slid down from the rock, still holding the rope.

Once on his feet, he shook the rope free of any obstruc-

tion so that it would fall easily to the ground. He tied the
loose end to a convenient pine and relaxed somewhat.

The Dream-horse jumped with alarm when Horse Seeker
stepped around the rock into sight. The animal whirled
to run but felt the restraining rope around his throat and
stopped short.

"It is good, my brother."

Horse Seeker was pleased once more. Secure in the
knowledge that the other end was tied fast, he took the
rope in his hand and tugged gently. After only a moment's hesitation, the horse took a step toward him. *Aiee,*
this was going well!

Summoning his courage, Horse Seeker untied the rope
from the tree and stood face-to-face with the Dream-
horse, only the slender rope between them. Some time
was required, and much patience, for him to coax the
horse to the spring to drink.

Once the animal was startled at some imagined danger
and sprang away. Horse Seeker braced himself for the
shock at the end of the rope. At the first tightening,
however, the horse stopped and stood, rolling white-
rimmed eyes in excitement but understanding the restraint of the rawhide line.

The Dream-horse drank deeply and stood with droplets
spilling from his lips. Then he turned to look again at his
captor.

"It is good, Dream-horse," the youth crooned softly.
"Now come."

Slowly and patiently he led the horse again to the
rocks where their medicine together had begun.

"You must stay here for now, my friend."

To avoid the risk of tangling the rope during his absence, Horse Seeker climbed the rock and tied it firmly
to the limb above once more. Again he brought food for
the horse. Then he left the canyon, jogging toward his
meeting with Yellow Bird. He smiled as he ran. There
would be much to tell her.

Yellow Bird and her father were already waiting when
Horse Seeker arrived. The young man was not surprised.
Surely a man such as Spotted Elk would wish to see for
himself the things told by his daughter.

Horse Seeker waved a greeting, and, before he spoke, his broad smile told Yellow Bird of his success.

"You have captured your Dream-horse!"

"Yes! Come and see. Spotted Elk, welcome!"

He turned and led the way, the horses of the others following closely. He was amused by the excited chatter of Yellow Bird but was scarcely less excited himself.

As they neared the canyon, he paused.

"Maybe we should leave your horses here."

Spotted Elk nodded and swung down. He had said very little, Horse Seeker noticed. No matter, he would soon speak.

The three proceeded on foot, slowing their stride as they approached the pole gate. Inside, horses raised their heads to look curiously. Spotted Elk's mouth dropped open as he stared.

"*Aiee*," he muttered at last, "these are the finest mares I have ever seen. Your elk-dog medicine is strong!"

Horse Seeker was almost too flattered to answer but managed to take best advantage of the situation.

"They are yours, Uncle. Except for the Dream-horse and the black mare, I give them all to you. I ask for your daughter, Yellow Bird, as my wife."

27

》》》

Horse Seeker was half afraid that Spotted Elk would be reluctant to lose his daughter. It had been easy to see that the chief had not wholeheartedly approved of the young stranger.

But now Spotted Elk's attitude had changed. Yellow Bird must have told her father a great deal about Horse Seeker's mission. There was a glint of admiration and even respect now as he looked at the younger man. It was without hesitation, then, that he gave permission for the two to marry.

"Of course, Horse Seeker. I welcome you to my lodge."

This, the young man realized, referred to a custom of the River People. A newly married couple moved into the lodge of the girl's parents until they were able to establish their own. It was much the same among his own people.

Horse Seeker nodded.

"It is good. Only not now. I must stay here and strengthen my medicine with the Dream-horse. Come, I will show you."

The three climbed into the enclosure. Cautioned by Horse Seeker, they approached the tethered stallion.

"We must stay back. I have not yet touched him."

The red stallion stood, excited, trembling a little, but proud and tall.

"Truly," Spotted Elk said softly, "here is the chief of all elk-dogs. Come, we must not alarm him."

Again there was the hint of admiration and respect in Spotted Elk's glance as he looked at the future husband of his daughter.

They climbed over the barrier and moved back to where the horses were tied. There were plans to be made.

After long talk, it was decided that the three would herd the mare band back to the village. Then Horse Seeker would return to continue his medicine with the Dream-horse. There would be no mention of this to the rest of the River People. It would be told that Horse Seeker had returned bringing horses for the father of Yellow Bird. He would come again soon for the marriage.

Meanwhile, the Dream-horse and the plans of Horse Seeker would be known only to the lodge of Spotted Elk. Bright Leaf, of course, would be told, but it was essential to the plan that the Dream-horse be a complete surprise to all, both the River People and the Blue Paints.

These things agreed, the three returned to the canyon. The black mare was tied near the Dream-horse to reassure him. Horse Seeker would ride the spotted mare.

It was with some misgiving that Horse Seeker raised the heavy gate. The other two were mounted and ready when he bunched the mare band together and drove them into the open. Quickly, Spotted Elk and the girl began to circle the group, turning back any who sought to escape. Horse Seeker dropped the barrier back in place, untied the black mare to roam the enclosure, and mounted the spotted mare.

They began to drive the band steadily, but with no hurry, in the general direction they wished. One flighty young mare and her foal kept trying to break away. Spotted Elk called softly.

"Shall we let this one go? She could cause us to lose them all!"

Horse Seeker nodded agreement. Carefully, they allowed the one pair to separate from the rest and moved on.

Things moved more smoothly without the exciting influence of the nervous mare. Even so, it was nearly dark when they reached the village. They pushed the newcomers into a meadow where the horses of the River People already grazed. The animals began to move among the others, pausing to snatch mouthfuls of the lush grass.

Horse Seeker rode alongside Yellow Bird.

"You know that I must go back."

"Yes, I know."

"Will you come soon?"

"Of course. I will bring food. Three suns?"

He nodded. The parting seemed more difficult than ever. There were many things to talk of, plans to make.

"I will look for you. Come to the canyon now, not the hill."

"It is good."

He paid his respects to her father, and they parted once more. But not for long, he told himself as he traveled through the night back to the canyon. Soon we will be together.

Reaching the canyon, Horse Seeker went directly to see that the stallion was safe. He spent a short while talking soothingly to the nervous Dream-horse, then sought his robe. He must be rested for the coming day.

Now the true strength of his medicine would be tested. He had not yet placed a hand on the glossy red coat of the Dream-horse.

It would be necessary to establish touch, both physically and in spirit. He must be able to communicate with the mind of the stallion, to get inside his head. Their thoughts must be as one.

With the rising of the sun, Horse Seeker approached the captive stallion. There was now no distraction from the milling herd. Only the black mare cropped grass quietly nearby. The spotted mare of Yellow Bird had been left outside the enclosure.

The young man walked directly toward the Dream-horse, slowly and with ceremony. The horse stood still, watching closely, yet unafraid.

At about three paces distance, Horse Seeker stopped and nodded a greeting, exactly as he would have greeted another person.

"*Ah-koh*, my friend. Now we will begin."

He began to sing the soft, soothing cadence already
familiar to the stallion. Now, however, there was a for-
mality, a ceremonial quality to the song. The singer
improvised as he proceeded yet adhered to time-honored
rhythm and tone, using all his skills as a medicine man
of the People.

> "I am sorry my brother,
> But I must ask your help.
> There is trouble among my people,
> And in the tribe of my friends.
> I need to borrow your strength
>   and your cunning.
> In exchange I offer the strength
>   of my medicine.
> We shall work together, you
>   and I,
> We shall borrow each other's
>   medicine
> For a little while."

The horse stood very still, ears pricked forward, alert.
The two looked into each other's eyes, and the whole
world seemed somewhere far away. There was stillness
in the canyon except for the sounds of the black mare's
feeding. Even the raucous cries from a crow circling
overhead seemed muted, in tune with the dreamy silence
that attended this ceremony.

Horse Seeker glanced upward at the bird and smiled
inwardly. He felt that his medicine was good.

28

>> >> >>

It was two suns before Horse Seeker touched the stallion. He continued to sing, to lead the animal to water and to graze. The routine became familiar to the two, a comfortable sequence of things, but now it was time for the next step.

> "Today, my brother,
> Today I ask you,
> Lend me your freedom
> For a little while."

He had led the animal to the spring and now paused in an open place, holding the rawhide rope. The Dreamhorse was leading easily now, understanding that the rope's restraint meant no threat. In fact, the presence of the man on the other end often signaled pleasant things, such as water and fresh grass.

But now Horse Seeker must use all his medicine. Hand over hand he moved up the rope, crooning softly. If the horse appeared nervous or excited, he paused, not moving until the stallion quieted. Closer and closer he ap-

proached, letting the Dream-horse catch his scent from
upwind. The animal blew noisily through flared nostrils,
testing the smell.

Carefully, Horse Seeker reached a hand forward, holding the rope in the other. The Dream-horse rolled his
eyes apprehensively and trembled, but he stood fast. When
the hand finally touched the glossy neck and no harm
came, the stallion began to relax.

> "You see, my brother,
> I mean you no harm."

He breathed slowly into the very nostrils of the horse,
sharing the breath of their lives. Then, gently, he began
the medicine of the ceremony. The horse's coat was
damp with sweat from excitement. Horse Seeker paused
to wipe sweat from his own brow with a finger, then
rubbed the finger along the horse's neck, mixing the
scents of the two. Next, he touched the flaring nostrils,
anointing their rims with the mixed odors.

> "You see, my brother,
> Our medicine mixes well.
> Together we will help each other
> To do many powerful things."

This seemed to have a calming effect. Soon, Horse
Seeker was stroking the shining coat, placing his hands
along the neck and shoulder. The trembling had stopped.

There remained one more step to complete the ritual.
Horse Seeker took a thong from his waist and allowed
the Dream-horse to smell it and become relaxed again.
The horse tested the rawhide with his lips, trying to
determine whether this was something to eat. Horse
Seeker slipped the thong between the teeth and smoothly
knotted it beneath the horse's jaw. Now the center of the
thong rested in a loop around the jaw, both ends dangling.

The influence of this loop circling the jaw had been
found to be powerful elk-dog medicine. The circle was a
copy of the most potent of all elk-dog medicines, the
Spanish ring bit. Horse Seeker had heard the tale, how
his grandfather, Heads Off, and Coyote, father of Tall

One, had adapted the medicine circle for use by the
People.

>"Now, my friend,
>The circle is finished.
>Our medicine never ends,
>But goes 'round forever."

He removed the rope from the horse's neck and now
led the animal freely with only the thong. The Dream-
horse worked tongue and mouth in a chewing motion,
tossing his head occasionally but tolerating the medicine
well.

Soon the stallion raised his head and nickered loudly.
An answering call came from the canyon's mouth, and
Horse Seeker waved a greeting to Yellow Bird. He led the
Dream-horse forward, proud to show their progress.

"*Aiee*, Horse Seeker, your medicine is strong! Already
your Dream-horse does your bidding!"

"No, no, we have only begun. I have not sat on the
back of the Dream-horse. There is much to do."

He knotted the dangling reins over the stallion's neck
and released the horse to graze, still in the enclosure. He
climbed over the gate to join Yellow Bird.

"Our plans go well, little one. As soon as I can ride the
Dream-horse, we will be married."

"You will ride him to the village?"

"No, there will be much more work to do. The horse
must still be secret, but I can leave him to attend a
marriage."

He smiled, then continued.

"If you still want me, of course."

The girl frowned as if this were a great decision.

"Well, perhaps. I have no better prospects," she spoke
to a nearby tree. "And this one has given my father many
horses. Oh, Horse Seeker! There is much talk of the
horses. None finer have been seen."

The young man smiled again.

"Wait until they see the Dream-horse!"

A frown clouded Yellow Bird's face.

"Must you fight Walks-Like-Thunder? I am afraid for
you. The River People can move away from the Blue
Paints' country. It has already been talked of."

"But I cannot, Yellow Bird. He carries the medicine of my people. I must recover it, even if I did not know you or the River People."

She nodded sadly, then brightened.

"Yes, I know. I only wished. But now, when will we be married?"

"Soon. Maybe seven suns. Then you can stay here with me!"

They laughed and chattered happily and planned where to place their temporary lodge, merely a skin cover over a sheltered area among the rocks. Finally it was time to part. Yellow Bird must return to the village.

The young man walked with her to her horse.

"You must take care. I do not like for you to ride alone."

"You sound like my father. I will be safe!"

She nudged her mount with a heel and cantered away. Horse Seeker watched her go, admiring the way she sat and rode. *Aiee*, all was going well! How could a young man be so fortunate as to have a wife like this one?

He worked with the Dream-horse a little longer, then began to settle in for the night. He sat by his fire, seeing pictures in its flickering coals, and finally rolled in his robe.

Sleep would not come. He was too excited. He watched the Seven Hunters circle the Real-star for a while. The spotted mare grazed quietly near him.

Then the mare raised her head, looking out across the plain to the south. She nickered softly, and somewhere a horse answered.

Horse Seeker glanced at his fire. It flickered lazily. He quickly decided that it was useless now to try to extinguish it. Whoever was approaching must have already seen its light. Instead, he tossed a couple of dry sticks on the glowing coals and retreated into the darkness. He gripped his bow and fitted an arrow to the string.

It seemed a long time that he listened to the soft clip-clop of the approaching horse before he could see the outline of the rider. The fire brightened, pushing back shadows as the new fuel ignited. The rider paused.

"Horse Seeker," he called. "Are you there? It is Spotted Elk!"

The young man stepped into the firelight, fear beginning to grip his stomach.

"Here, Uncle."

"Horse Seeker, is Yellow Bird with you? She has not returned."

29
>> >> >>

Yellow Bird hurried along the now familiar trail. She had stayed at the canyon somewhat longer than was wise. It had been so difficult to tear herself away. It had been such a happy time, the plans they had made together. Their joy in each other and in the coming marriage had overshadowed all concerns. Not only was it easy to forget Horse Seeker's primary mission, it was easy to forget danger.

The riders were some distance away when the girl first noticed them. She attempted to count them. Seven or eight. She could not be sure. They were well out on the gently sloping plain but headed directly for her.

Yellow Bird believed that they had not yet seen her. She reined aside to the west, hoping to lose herself in the broken foothills. She thumped the surprised horse firmly in the flank and sprinted up the slope. A scatter of pines spread up the hill ahead, and to this concealment she pointed her way. She reined to a stop and dismounted, holding the horse's muzzle to prevent its crying out to the approaching animals.

She had not yet identified the riders. It was possible, of

course, that it was a hunting party from her own band.
But no, she could see now that they were strangers. This
left little doubt. They were Blue Paints, eight of them.
Their leader was a large, burly man, and it took only the
space of a heartbeat to recognize the dreaded Walks-Like-
Thunder.

Yellow Bird tried to shrink back farther into the shadows. To her dismay, the approaching riders would cross
her trail almost at the point she had left it. Which way
would they turn? Or would they continue up the slope
toward her? It might be necessary to run for her life. If
she could elude the Blue Paints until she was near the
village, she might expect help from her people.

She now saw that the burly chief rode a gray horse.
This was not good. The gray was the prized mare of
Horse Seeker's people, said to be fast as the wind. If it
came to a chase, her horse could never outrun Gray
Cloud.

Now the riders had stopped, pointing and arguing. The
girl realized that they were examining her tracks. It would
be only a moment until they discovered the displaced
earth and pine needles where she had wheeled her horse
up the slope. She swung to the horse's back, ready to run.

A man called out excitedly, pointing at the ground and
then, to her horror, directly up the hill at the thicket
where she stood. The horse wheeled once more, pounding up the slope through the trees. Behind her, Yellow
Bird could hear the pounding of hooves, the shouts of
pursuers.

Her horse, not noted for his fleetness but sure of foot,
clattered across the loose rock of a shifting slide. Ahead,
a fallen pine lay across their path. The horse tucked his
forefeet neatly and jumped the obstacle. Too late, Yellow
Bird saw that there was no safe place to land on the other
side. The dim trail was satisfactory for the deer that used
it but not for a running horse. Broken rock and crevices
lay beyond the log.

She heard the bone snap as the left foreleg slipped into
a crevice. Then the horse was falling, and the girl was
thrown violently through the air, over the head of the
stricken animal. The rocky ground rushed up at her, and
the impact drove the breath from her lungs.

For a moment there was blackness. Her mind told her

she must get up, run, hide, try to escape, but her body refused to obey. With great effort she rolled to her back, gasping for breath. Oddly, she noticed how bright was the blue of the sky above her through the tops of the pines.

Her pursuers came and stood over her. She was dimly aware of their presence, but it seemed to lack meaning. They were talking, but the words made no sense.

"It is a girl!" One of the warriors exclaimed with astonishment.

"Is she dead?"

Walks-Like-Thunder shouldered his way forward and leaned over to glance at the crippled horse.

"Kill the elk-dog," he muttered. "At least we have meat."

"What of the girl?"

He stepped over to look down at the bloodied head of Yellow Bird.

"Kill her, too. She is probably too injured to live. She is of no use to us."

The young man nearest her bent to brush dirt and pine needles from her face.

"She is very pretty," he said wistfully. "Can we keep her alive tonight, my chief?"

Walks-Like-Thunder whirled on the young man.

"She is yours, Blue Jay," he pointed and spoke sternly. "We will wait until morning when we move on. Then I will decide."

"It is good, my chief."

Walks-Like-Thunder stalked away, then turned again.

"If she becomes any trouble, you will kill her then."

He shrugged and seemed to soften.

"Who knows? If she lives, she may be worth something."

The young man called Blue Jay carried the half-conscious girl to a more level spot. Around him, the others began to make camp for the night.

"Hey, Blue Jay, do you like your women half-dead?" someone called.

"That is the only kind that will sleep with him," answered another.

There was general laughter.

Blue Jay stood and held up a hand in protest.

"Our chief has said if she lives, she may be of some use."

At any rate, it might be worth a little effort. He had nothing to lose but a little sleep. Even if the girl died, he had lost nothing.

She stirred and moaned, and Blue Jay poured a little water from his waterskin into his palm to wet her face. She was very pretty. He hoped that she would not die during the night.

30
≫ ≫ ≫

When morning came, Blue Jay found the girl not only alive but staring at him with large dark eyes. He rose and stood near her, hesitant as to how to begin.

"You must get up," he used the sign talk.

"I cannot. I am injured."

"You must. Our chief has said if you are any trouble, he will kill you."

He pulled the girl to her feet as gently as he could, aware of the pain in her face. Walks-Like-Thunder stalked over and looked the prisoner up and down.

"So, she is still alive."

He roughly handled her arms and legs, searching for injuries. The girl winced but said nothing.

"No broken bones. But, she is yours, Blue Jay. Will she ride your horse while you walk?"

There was laughter. Yellow Bird did not understand the joke, but it appeared to be at the expense of her young captor.

"She can ride behind me, my chief."

Walks-Like-Thunder shook his head in consternation.

"She must not slow our travel, Blue Jay. If she does, I will kill her myself."

He looked again at the slim figure of the prisoner.

"A bit thin for my choice in bed," he muttered, as he walked toward the horses.

"Listen, girl," Blue Jay signed rapidly. "You must ride behind me, even if you hurt. Our chief says if you delay us, he will kill you."

The girl nodded. This was far different from the childish fantasies of capture by the Blue Paints that she and Pretty Basket had shared. Besides, she hurt. Each movement brought a wave of pain across her back, chest, everywhere. She took a deep breath, hurting tender ribs again. She must make the best of this and look for chances to escape. She turned to her captor, the young warrior who had spoken in the sign talk.

"How are you called?"

"I am Blue Jay," he smiled.

"And I am Yellow Bird."

The sign for "bird" brought a jab of pain to the muscles of her shoulder, but she continued.

"Where are we going?"

"Who knows? We are on a hunting party but have found nothing except your horse. He was tough to chew."

"Where are your people?"

Yellow Bird hoped to establish a communication of sorts with this young man. It was good to have a friend among her enemies.

However, the question proved fruitless. Blue Jay only shrugged noncommittally.

Now people were preparing to mount. Blue Jay beckoned to her and led her to a rawboned gelding. He swung up and reached a hand to the girl. Every bone and joint hurt as he swung her up behind him. It was all she could do to keep from crying out. Only the thought of Blue Jay's warning made her silently clench her teeth and settle to the horse's rump behind him. She had noticed the massive stone club that dangled at the waist of Walks-Like-Thunder.

The course of the party seemed aimless. They appeared to be simply wandering, hoping to encounter game.

Yellow Bird knew that game had been plentiful this year. Her own people had found many deer, elk, and buffalo without even moving their camp. It must be the same with the Blue Paints. This party, then, was only half serious in the hunt. Their dual purpose would include the possibility of scouting for future raids against the River People. If they encountered a lone hunter, such as they had first thought her to be, it could provide amusement to chase and capture or kill.

One thing bothered the girl. There had been no attempt to question her. They must have thought her in extremely poor condition. She realized that she had been unconsious, or only semiconscious, for some time. In fact, she remembered little of the night.

During a rest stop, Walks-Like-Thunder approached the place where she sat with Blue Jay.

"You, girl," he began with sign talk. "Where are your people?"

Yellow Bird thought rapidly. The Blue Paints would have knowledge of her people's whereabouts. It would do no good to lie.

"They are still where we spent the winter."

She pointed, as accurately as she could. The chief's nod said that he believed her to be telling the truth. Then his expression became crafty.

"Why do you ride alone?"

Walks-Like-Thunder had apparently realized that here was an unusual circumstance. A girl should not have been riding alone, as they had found her. The enemy chief now suspected something.

A moment of panic seized her. She must protect Horse Seeker at all costs. If her answer was unconvincing, they might even return to backtrack her trail to the canyon where the Dream-horse was held.

She paused, stammering, embarrassed. Careful, she told herself. This must look right.

"Where do you ride?"

The expression on the dark face of Walks-Like-Thunder was now urgent and threatening as he repeated his question. Yellow Bird burst into tears.

"To meet my lover!" She signed frantically. "My father hates him, and we meet in secret."

There was laughter. One of the men who had been watching used sign talk for a ribald comment.

"You need no lover now," he leered. "You can have all of us!"

More laughter. Yellow Bird pretended not to understand.

"My chief!" Blue Jay spoke in their own tongue, indignantly. "You said the girl belongs to me!"

"Yes, yes, Blue Jay. She is yours."

The chief dismissed the matter with a wave of the hand.

Yellow Bird did not understand this last exchange, but she realized that the situation had relaxed. The Blue Paints had accepted her story of a secret lover. She smiled to herself. This would prevent the scouting party from searching further for her reasons for riding alone.

The party prepared to move on, and Yellow Bird cringed again with pain as she swung up behind Blue Jay.

31

>> >> >>

Horse Seeker and Spotted Elk were following the girl's trail as soon as there was enough light. They found the place where she turned aside and were dismayed to see the trampling tracks of several horsemen.

The two men urged their horses up the hill, dreading what they might find. Only now did Horse Seeker notice a pair of circling buzzards overhead. The horses clattered across a shifting rock slope. From a clump of pines ahead, another buzzard flapped away in alarm.

It took only a short while to read the signs. The dead and butchered horse, campfires of six or eight men. To the great relief of both, there was no sign of the girl's body. She must be still alive, even though a prisoner.

A bit more deliberate tracking was required to find the direction of the party's departure. They seemed to be wandering aimlessly. Apparently this was a hunting or scouting party. There was no way of knowing their identity, but both men knew the likeliest possibility—the Blue Paints. They pushed on.

"Horse Seeker," the girl's father mused during one brief stop, "what if we do find them? What then?"

"I do not know, my chief. We must first find them,
then make plans."

Spotted Elk had grave reservations. What could two
men do against a party of the Blue Paints? But, of course,
the young man was right. First they must find the captors of the girl. Spotted Elk devoutly hoped that the
medicine of Horse Seeker was as strong as his daughter
believed.

Shadows were growing long before the riders were lo-
cated. The two men paused as Spotted Elk held up his
hand.

"Horse Seeker! Do you smell the smoke?"

The other nodded.

"They are stopping for the night."

"Now what?"

"My chief, we cannot fight this many Blue Paints.
They would only kill us."

Spotted Elk nodded. He was not a coward, but only
practical.

"So," Horse Seeker continued, "let us ride in openly to
talk."

It seemed a reasonable approach. Protocol demanded a
certain courtesy to persons approaching one's camp. An
overt act by the Blue Paints would be strictly against
custom. This approach would allow them to evaluate
their adversaries and determine the condition of the girl.

Horse Seeker took a deep breath and kneed his mount
forward. The two rode slowly, in plain sight in the open.
There must be no misunderstanding here. At best, the
situation was risky. Side by side, they moved toward the
camp of the Blue Paints.

Now the flicker of campfires could be seen, and pun-
gent pine smoke drifted across the slope like a wisp of
fog. Several men moved among the trees, gathering fuel.
It could have been any routine stopping place for any of
the tribes.

But it was not. A warrior noticed the advancing
horsemen and dropped his armful of sticks. He cried a
warning as he reached for the weapon at his waist.

Spotted Elk and Horse Seeker stopped and waited. Both
raised empty right hands, palm forward, indicating the
universal sign "I have no weapon."

Men came running, and the two moved forward again.

Ahead, Horse Seeker saw the slim form of Yellow Bird. She had been tending one of the fires but now straightened to look anxiously toward them. His mind was racing. How could they barter, strike some sort of exchange for her release? His heart sank as he realized that neither he or Spotted Elk carried anything of value with which to bargain.

A burly man rose from a sitting position and strode forward. With a shock, Horse Seeker recognized the dreaded Blue Paint chief.

"Walks-Like-Thunder!"

Spotted Elk had also identified the leader of the party.

"It is not good, Horse Seeker."

Now was a time to think rapidly and act very slowly. Horse Seeker realized that he had created a very difficult situation. At their last meeting, he had insulted the Blue Paint chief and promised to meet him in combat. This encounter might be interpreted as the culmination of his boast.

If so, the situation was completely hopeless. He rode the girl's horse and carried borrowed weapons. He was completely unprepared for action of the sort required to meet the mighty Walks-Like-Thunder. Both he and Spotted Elk would be killed, and Yellow Bird would spend the rest of her life as a slave-wife among the Blue Paints.

For a moment, he wondered what would become of the Dream-horse, imprisoned in the hidden canyon. *Aiee*, that had been progressing so well. But it would take many days more until the Dream-horse became a war-horse under his medicine.

Then Horse Seeker saw the answer to the problem. Straight toward Walks-Like-Thunder he rode, his mind racing ahead. Stopping directly before the surprised chief, Horse Seeker raised a hand in greeting and began the sign talk without further ceremony.

"Blue Paint, I come to challenge you."

There was a muffled sound at his elbow which may have been a gasp of surprise from Spotted Elk. Yellow Bird stood at a little distance, a look of shocked horror frozen on her face. She did not move closer but glanced around for a weapon in case it became necessary. Behind the girl, Horse Seeker saw a young warrior move toward her.

The burly chief stood silent only a moment, then threw back his head and laughed uproariously. He reached for his heavy war club.

"This will soon be finished," he chuckled.

"No, my chief," Horse Seeker signaled formally. "Not now. I have only a borrowed horse. We will meet at the Moon of Thunder."

He had calculated carefully. It was not yet the Moon of Roses. By the Thunder Moon there should be enough time to finish the teaching of the Dream-horse.

"I will meet you at this spot," he continued, "and recover what is mine."

Walks-Like-Thunder insolently flipped the dangling Spanish bit which hung around his neck.

"This trinket? You will have to take it from my neck."

"In time, Thunder. For now, let its medicine weaken you a little longer. Already you can only fight women."

He indicated Yellow Bird.

"This woman also belongs to me. There is also the matter of my horse."

He had seen the gray tied among the pines.

Walks-Like-Thunder laughed again.

"You will have to take the horse from under me. The woman is not my problem. She belongs to Blue Jay there."

Horse Seeker was tempted to challenge the young warrior on the spot, but it would not be prudent. For now, he would have to be content with the knowledge that the girl was alive and not badly injured. He looked across at the glowering Blue Jay.

"I will deal with you later," he promised. "I hold you for her safety."

The only answer was an obscene gesture from Blue Jay.

Walks-Like-Thunder was not finished.

"This challenge," he resumed. "Why have it here? Let us meet at the Medicine Rocks and bring both tribes to watch."

Horse Seeker was not familiar with the area. In each part of the country were places called by such names. He turned a questioning look to Spotted Elk.

"It is good, Horse Seeker. We know the place."

The young man nodded, then signaled to the Blue Paint.

"Good. But only we two are to fight? No battle?"

"Yes." Walks-Like-Thunder chuckled again. "All can watch."

He turned to look at Yellow Bird.

"Even the woman of Blue Jay can watch you be killed. This will be the Moon of Walks-Like-Thunder."

The last picture in the mind of Horse Seeker as he turned to ride away was the slim figure of Yellow Bird standing tall in the firelight. Her eyes followed him, and her spirit reached out toward him, confident in his ability to help her.

His heart was heavy.

32

》》》

"**W**ill there be enough time to teach your Dream-horse?"

Spotted Elk was concerned.

Both men looked back on the confrontation with mixed feelings as they rode away. They had not managed to free the girl. Still, they now knew that she was alive and relatively uninjured. They had identified her captors, and the time was now set for the combat between Horse Seeker and the Blue Paint chief.

There was much advantage to the coming event in the Moon of Thunder. By establishing this thing to look forward to, much of the risk of small raids by the Blue Paints was eliminated.

Horse Seeker hesitated long before answering the question posed by the older man. Would there be enough time?

"*Aiee,* I hope so!"

If not, he reminded himself, it would result not only in his own death but perhaps in that of many others, as Walks-Like-Thunder continued his marauding. Yellow Bird would remain as the wife of a Blue Paint.

Equally important to his people as a group, their elk-dog medicine would be lost forever. Horse Seeker did not wish to speculate on whether the Elk-dog People could survive without it.

They rode through the night for some time without speaking. The young man did not know how to voice his concerns. Finally he spoke, tentatively.

"Spotted Elk, my heart is heavy for Yellow Bird."

"Mine also, my son."

"I wish she could be freed."

He reined his horse in a trifle, as if to return.

"No, Horse Seeker. It is not to be. I, too, would wish it. But you see how angry is the spirit of Walks-Like-Thunder. If we try to release her, he would kill her. For now, she is safe."

"But, Uncle, what of the man, Blue Jay, who claims her?"

"That is good. If she belongs to him, he will protect her. She will not be abused by all the men."

"But, I—"

"Horse Seeker," the older man continued firmly, "he will see that she is well treated. If he wants her for himself, it helps him to do so. If he hopes to sell her, or ransom her, she will bring more if she is in good condition."

The stark reality of this situation had been unspoken until now. The words of Spotted Elk clawed at the heart of the young man, but he knew that they were true. It had been a long speech for Spotted Elk, and a difficult one. To see his daughter as a captive of the enemy had not been an easy thing, Horse Seeker knew.

They rode without speaking for a time until Spotted Elk broke the silence with a chuckle, completely startling his companion.

"Horse Seeker," the older man mused, "how would you like to try to hold that girl against her will?"

The young man thought for a few moments. Yes, Spotted Elk was right. The man, Blue Jay, would certainly have his problems. To control this strong-willed young woman, who was also resourceful and intelligent, would be a difficult thing.

The idea became more amusing as he thought about it, and soon the two were chuckling together. It was not from lack of concern. There was simply nothing that

they could accomplish, and they must either laugh or
cry. Horse Seeker would do both in the coming days.

"Now, how can I help you prepare for the Moon of
Thunder?"

Horse Seeker thought for some time before answering.

"There is little anyone can do except the Dream-horse
and me. I will need weapons."

"What will you use?"

"A lance. Yes, that will be good. Can this be done?"

"Of course. A shield, also?"

"No, I need both hands. A light axe?"

"Yes, Horse Seeker, it will be done. I will bring them
to your canyon."

"And tell no one. The surprise is one of my weapons!"

They were nearing the place where they would part.

"Yes," nodded Spotted Elk. "I will say that Yellow Bird
has been stolen by the Blue Paints and that we will meet
them later to talk of ransom. Of course, I must tell her
mother."

"Of course."

"Shall I bring you food?"

"No, I can hunt."

He held up the bow, then continued.

"That may become part of the Dream-horse's training."

Spotted Elk nodded. He turned and started away, then
paused.

"Horse Seeker," he began tentatively, "do not be sad.
Yellow Bird is safe."

"I know, Uncle, but my heart cries for her."

He reined the spotted mare aside and rode away without looking back. He did not entirely see how all things
would manage to work themselves out.

There were the two entirely separate problems, that of
the Blue Paint chief and the appointed combat, obviously
to the death. Then there was the matter of young Blue
Jay. Must he also fight this man for possession of the
girl?

These answers would come in time, but it was hard to
be patient. He could not bear the thoughts of Yellow Bird
in the embrace of the Blue Paint.

Aiee, the time would be long and lonely until the
Moon of Thunder.

33
>> >> >>

Yellow Bird watched the darkness close around the
departing figures of her father and Horse Seeker. She
stood still, silent and unmoving. She must be strong
now.

Her mind moved rapidly. She had seen the entire exchange of sign talk and grasped the reasons for the challenge. Now the time was set. She could look forward to
release in the Moon of Thunder. Just how that might
come about, she could not be sure. It was enough to
know that Horse Seeker knew her whereabouts. He would
find a way.

The immediate problem which faced her was that of
her captor, Blue Jay. Actually she was grateful to him. He
had been kind to her, and by claiming her as his property
he had established a certain degree of protection. It was
not unheard of for a woman captured by the Blue Paints
to be repeatedly raped by the entire party and then killed
or left to die from the abuse.

But now, as the property of Blue Jay, she would not be
subjected to such violation by the others without his
permission. She must tread a narrow trail now. She must

be friendly enough to the young warrior to retain his protection. At the same time, she had no desire to become his wife.

She gave a sidelong glance at Blue Jay. He continually hovered near her. Yellow Bird groaned softly and bent forward, then straightened. She must keep him thinking that her injuries were more severe than they actually were. This might postpone for some time the inevitable demand that she join him in bed.

It was not hard to feign her injuries. Every part of her body ached, both from the fall and the day's punishing travel.

At the same time, Yellow Bird knew she must not irritate her captor. Even though Blue Jay now saw himself as her protector, his mood could change. At any moment, he could grow tired of the game. If she became a nuisance to carry on the horse behind him, he could simply abandon her on the plain.

That would be acceptable. She could survive. What worried her was the threat of the chief to kill her if she became a problem. Blue Jay, too, or any of the other men in the party could kill her in a sudden fit of anger, to argue about it later.

Yes, she must do her best to appear friendly and cooperative yet partially incapacitated. She smiled weakly at Blue Jay, who now initiated conversation in sign talk.

"So that is your lover?"

It was a statement, rather than a question, and was accompanied by a sneer.

Yellow Bird nodded weakly, groaned a little, and sat down. Now was the time to appear weak and incapable.

"How far must we travel to your people?"

She rubbed a sore spot on her hip.

"Two, three sleeps."

Good. She was making progress. He had refused to answer this question previously. But now Blue Jay pursued his conversation.

"You will see your lover killed," he sneered.

Yellow Bird did not answer.

"No one can stand before Walks-Like-Thunder."

He was determined to taunt her with this idea, she saw. She must show a little spirit to make her attitude believable. She raised her head.

"But if he does kill Walks-Like-Thunder, I go free?"

For the first time since she had known him, Blue Jay laughed.

"Of course not," he strutted. "Then he must fight me."

The young warrior apparently felt safe in his boast. There was little likelihood that anyone would survive combat with Walks-Like-Thunder.

The girl had noticed that again Horse Seeker had attempted to plant seeds of doubt among the Blue Paints.

"You must fight him, then," she stated flatly. "By the Moon of Thunder, your chief may be dead. Horse Seeker's medicine weakens him each day."

She indicated the dangling metal ornament around the chief's burly neck.

There was a moment of hesitation, a fleeting doubt on the part of Blue Jay. The girl pushed her slight advantage.

"None of you knows the danger you face. Horse Seeker carries powerful medicine from a far tribe."

Walks-Like-Thunder swaggered over, planted his feet, and glared at her.

"Silence, woman!"

He took the Spanish bit between thumb and forefinger and wiggled it before her.

"This is only a bauble. Your lover's medicine is weak. You are our prisoner, and I will kill him in the Moon of Thunder."

He whirled on his heel to stalk away. Yellow Bird realized that she had struck a tender spot. She could not resist one final jibe.

"You have tried, before," she called after him.

The retort was in her own tongue and was not understood by any of the listeners, but Walks-Like-Thunder turned back. He faced Blue Jay and almost shouted at him. His meaning was clear.

Blue Jay hastily motioned to his prisoner to be still. It was well, she realized, that the chief had not understood. His tirade at her captor was obviously something like "you keep that girl quiet!"

Yellow Bird lowered her eyes and smiled quietly to herself. She was finding the things that were pleasing to her captors and those that were irritating.

She knew that there would be hard times between now

and the Moon of Thunder. The Blue Paints were said to
have far less regard for women than her own people.
Even less for captive women, she was certain.

Yet she believed she could survive the coming days. It
was not long until the meeting in combat of Horse Seeker
with the Blue Paint. She could exist in the knowledge
that the time of her rescue was coming.

Meanwhile, it might even be amusing to inject an
occasional taunt about the strength of Horse Seeker's
medicine. Any doubt on the part of the Blue Paints would
be useful.

As for herself, she had no doubts whatever. The strength
of the elk-dog medicine of Horse Seeker had been proven.
He had captured the legendary Fire-horse, the Dream-
horse of his vision.

Now, as the time approached for his fight to the death
with Walks-Like-Thunder, she was completely confident.
In fact, she more than half believed the taunt she had
thrown at the Blue Paints. She fully expected to watch
Walks-Like-Thunder weaken in the coming days from
the effect of the stolen medicine that he wore.

34
>> >> >>

Yellow Bird learned quickly not to do anything to upset or irritate the Blue Paint women.

When the scouting party arrived at the village, she had been thrust roughly toward one of the lodges. It was, she learned, that of the parents of Blue Jay.

The young man's father had three wives. The oldest, tall and dignified, appeared to be the main, or sit-by, wife. She was also the mother of Blue Jay. The others were younger, one fat and jolly, the other pretty and shy. Each cradled a small baby, and another youngster wandered around the lodge.

It became immediately apparent that the women expected the newcomer to do much of their work. Despite her injuries and her exaggerated limp, she was forced to carry wood and water. If she moved too slowly, she received blows from the other women, while any men nearby laughed and made jokes.

Yellow Bird did not object to the work. She was accustomed to it. She was not prepared for the manner in which the Blue Paint men treated their women. Almost routine things were shouts, orders, sometimes blows from the men administered to their own women, even. To the newcomer, this made no sense at all.

It was not long until she realized that, having no recourse, the Blue Paint women merely passed on the constant abuse. Lesser wives, children, prisoners, dogs, all received a share of shouts and blows.

It was much safer to do the bidding of the women. Yellow Bird did, however, note that the occasional taunt she was able to throw at the men did not go unnoticed. A jibe which made a man uncomfortable was accepted with amusement by the other women. Yellow Bird began to use her observations. She could stay on the good side of the women by working hard and doing their bidding. By showing a little defiance to their men, she kept them amused and relaxed.

The men, in turn, were perpetually on the edge of irritation. Yellow Bird taunted the burly chief at every opportunity. It was in subtle ways. To be too flagrant was dangerous. She would ask Walks-Like-Thunder, using the sign talk, how he was feeling or how his medicine was progressing.

Once she nearly went too far, and the chief strode toward her with arm raised to strike. The other women intervened, berating her and pushing her toward the lodge, away from Walks-Like-Thunder. As it happened, the only blows which actually struck her were slight, administered by the women. Once inside the lodge, there was much quiet giggling, while Walks-Like-Thunder stalked away. Again, Yellow Bird felt the strange cohesion among the women in quiet defiance of their men. Now, as a woman, she was almost included.

Dealing with Blue Jay was a more difficult matter. For many days, she avoided his advances by limping and pretending injury. From time to time, he made hints and suggestions, but she was able to refuse. She continued to sleep near him in the lodge, but wrapped in a separate robe.

Then came the day at the stream. Yellow Bird was a little apart from the other women and was standing in water above her knees, bathing. Her buckskin dress was draped over a nearby willow.

Blue Jay sauntered into sight from behind the bush.

Apparently he had been watching for some time. He eyed her long body appreciatively, then began sign talk.

"You are not injured." His stare was accusing.

"I am healing now." Yellow Bird's mind raced ahead. She dreaded the next conclusion on the part of Blue Jay. It was simple and to the point.

"You will come tonight to my bed."

It was not a question but a demand. Yellow Bird hesitated only a moment.

"Of course." She paused, appeared puzzled, and then continued with a question.

"It does not matter that I am unclean?"

Blue Jay's face changed. The hungry expression he had had as his eyes roved over her body was gone. Now there was almost a revulsion as he looked at her.

Yellow Bird had gambled. She did not know the customs of the Blue Paints but assumed that they would have many of the same taboos as other tribes. Among the strongest of these was that of menstrual uncleanliness.

If a woman touched the weapons of her husband during this time, they might be ruined. The bow would never be as strong; the arrows would never fly straight again. Some tribes, she knew, banished unclean women to a special menstrual lodge to avoid the dangers of contact with them.

Apparently she had hit upon a strict taboo of these people. Blue Jay was backing away, caught completely off guard by her innocent query. He looked confused, inexperienced. She could almost feel sorry for him.

"No, no," Blue Jay signed. "Not tonight, then. Later."

He retreated several steps, then turned and hurried away. Yellow Bird was relieved, amused, yet concerned. It had been a trick of the moment, and it had been effective. But for how long? This could delay the young man's advances only for a few days. The time of reckoning would come eventually.

She estimated on her fingers. It was at least ten days until her actual time would come. Until then, she would postpone as best she could.

It was three days before Blue Jay accosted her again.

"Your unclean time is past?"

"No, not yet."

The youg man appeared disappointed but accepted her answer.

A few days later, he was not so cooperative. He shook his head at her answer to the same question.

"This cannot be," he stated flatly. "The time is too long."

Yellow Bird flared in anger.

"I know it has been too long, stupid one! I have not been right since my horse fell with me. Here, do you want to take the risk?"

She started to pull up her buckskin dress as if to remove it over her head. The two were standing outside the lodge, and her angry outburst had attracted the attention of several passersby.

"Put your dress on," demanded the embarrassed Blue Jay.

Yellow Bird dropped the fringe of her dress, whirled, and ducked through the door into the lodge. Outside, she could hear the chuckles of amusement from those who had seen the exchange. The time was coming, she feared, when her deceit would be no longer successful. Again, she tried to count the days.

It was only the following day, however, when Blue Jay accosted her again outside the lodge.

"I do not believe you," he stated flatly. "You are not unclean."

She was about to react, but Blue Jay was continuing.

"The women will see!"

He motioned her inside the lodge, where the two young wives waited. Now she had no longer any way to avoid her captor's attentions.

Reluctantly, she lifted her skirt for the two women to examine her. She felt like a horse being examined before a trade. The fat one curiously touched the inside of Yellow Bird's thigh.

"It is as she says, Blue Jay!" she called through the doorway. "She is unclean!"

Astonished, the girl let her dress fall around her legs again. The woman was supporting her story, for reasons not entirely clear to Yellow Bird. She smiled her thanks.

The other of the two young women bore a disgruntled expression on her face. It was obvious that this one had cooperated against her better judgment. Yellow Bird must be very cautious now.

Secretly, she felt that time was on her side. She was feeling the unmistakable symptoms, the heaviness, the tenderness in her breasts. It could not be more than a day or two until her claim of menstruation became a fact.

She stepped outside to face the disappointed Blue Jay. A new possibility had occurred to her.

"It is as I said," she reminded him, using sign talk. "Now hear. I belong to Horse Seeker, but the Moon of Thunder is near. Let us wait until then. If your chief kills Horse Seeker, I will be your wife. But if he lives, it is between the two of you."

Yellow Bird realized that she had no bargaining power to speak of except her cooperation. Still, it would do no harm to try.

Blue Jay stood thinking for a moment. There was no doubt that Walks-Like-Thunder would crush the upstart. It would be far better to have the beautiful prisoner as a cooperative wife than as a defiant one. Such a spirited girl might even be dangerous later. He could wait a little longer.

"Agreed," he nodded.

35

» » »

Horse Seeker placed the three lances on the ground in front of him. He studied them carefully, comparing their proportions. Finally, he chose the longest of the three, lifted it, and hefted it for balance. Spotted Elk stood watching.

"No, not this one," Horse Seeker spoke. "It is good. It would be good for hunting but not for this, I think. There is too much bend."

He shook the long shaft of the lance, holding it at the point of balance. He could feel the slight, willowy spring of the weapon. No, it would not do. There must be more stiffness.

He pointed to the lances still on the ground.

"Not the short one. There would be no balance."

Horse Seeker lifted the remaining lance and smiled. Ah, this was a weapon! One could tell by the feel, heft, and balance whether the spirit of the object would be true. And this feel was good.

Horse Seeker smiled broadly.

"Yes, this is the one."

"It is good. And the axe?"

Horse Seeker took the weapon that the older man handed him. It was a lighter, trimmer version of the implement he had used to cut pines for poles. The handle was longer to give more reach for fighting hand to hand.

"It will do, Spotted Elk. With good medicine, I will not need it."

Privately he thought that if he were forced to face the might of the massive Blue Paint chief, one axe would be as good as another. The object of the fight would be to prevent such a confrontation. His plan to use the superior strength of the great red horse must be effective.

"Does your Dream-horse do well?" Spotted Elk was asking.

"Very well, Uncle. I will show you."

He led the way to the enclosure. It was now several suns since the two had parted. Spotted Elk had returned to bring the weapons. Meanwhile, Horse Seeker had pushed ahead with the stallion's training.

"Have you sat upon his back?"

Horse Seeker nodded.

"Only yesterday."

He stood inside the enclosure and whistled a low, soothing sound. The horse, grazing near the spring, raised his head, ears pointed forward. He trotted to the young man and stood, peering curiously. Horse Seeker, talking and crooning softly, stepped forward with hand outstretched. The Dream-horse sniffed the hand, blowing noisily through dilated nostrils.

When the time seemed right, Horse Seeker slipped a thong into the animal's mouth and deftly knotted it. He held the thong while he stroked and rubbed the animal's entire body and legs. He paid special attention to one favorite spot on the horse's withers, scratching while the animal stretched in pure ecstasy.

Next he rested his arms heavily on the horse's back, waiting until the stallion quieted again. Finally he swung up to sit on the powerful back. As he threw his leg across, the horse jumped excitedly and ran a few steps but then quieted. Horse Seeker continued to talk and sing softly and soothingly.

In a few moments, he began to urge the horse back and forth with gentle motions of the rawhide rein, with a light touch of knee or heel, and with subtle changes in the balance of his body. At last he swung to the ground and released the rawhide rein.

"*Aiee*," exclaimed Spotted Elk, "your medicine is strong."

Horse Seeker was pleased but knew that there was more involved.

"Yes, Uncle, but this is also a very wise horse. Sometimes, he knows already what I will do next."

Spotted Elk nodded.

"You will be ready?"

"I think so. But I will need someone now to help me."

"I will come."

"No, my chief. Some trusted young man who can stay here with me. Black Otter?"

"Yes," nodded the other. "What do you wish him to do?"

"Together we will teach the Dream-horse combat."

"Ah yes. It is good."

"This will help the Dream-horse become used to other people."

"Then you will bring the horse to our camp?"

Horse Seeker thought a long time, then spoke slowly.

"No, I think not. Listen, Uncle, why not a complete surprise at the start of the fight? This would put the Blue Paints off balance."

"You mean, hide the Dream-horse?"

"No. I will come to the Medicine Rocks after everyone else. Black Otter can show me the way. Your people can already be camped there."

Spotted Elk smiled. This appealed to his sense of humor. He could envision the suspense, the question whether Horse Seeker would appear at all. Then the astonishment at his appearance on the great red chief of all elk-dogs. It would be good. He began to think of ways to make the occasion even more striking.

"Yes, Horse Seeker, that is a good plan. When the time is right, I will take the River People to the Medicine Rocks. Then in two, three suns, you can follow."

He picked up the two rejected lances and started toward his horse. Then he paused and turned again.

"When do you want me to bring Black Otter?"

"Give me a little more time with the horse. Three suns."

Spotted Elk swung to his horse's back and waved a good-bye as he rode away.

Horse Seeker turned again to the Dream-horse.

"My brother," he spoke earnestly, "we have much to do."

36

>> >> >>

Black Otter sat on his horse, hands upon the withers, and stared, openmouthed. Then he began to laugh.

"This is the great secret, Uncle?" he spoke to Spotted Elk beside him.

"Yes," the older man nodded. "We could tell no one."

Horse Seeker waved from within the enclosure and came forward, leading the Dream-horse.

"*Aiee*, my friend, surely yours is the greatest of all elk-dog medicine," Black Otter murmured in delighted disbelief.

He swung down and went to meet Horse Seeker, still chuckling.

"This will be a glorious surprise for the Blue Paints."

"Move slowly," Horse Seeker cautioned. "He is still learning to trust."

"Your progress goes well, Horse Seeker?" Spotted Elk was asking.

"Yes, Uncle. We have done much since you left."

It was true. Horse Seeker could scarcely believe the rapid progress. He vaulted to the animal's back to illustrate, slid back over the rump, then mounted from the

159

opposite side and nudged the shiny flank to urge the horse into a sprint. After a circle of the enclosed canyon, he brought the Dream-horse to a sliding stop at the gate and leaped to the ground. He dropped one rein and spoke a single word, pointing to the spot where the rawhide touched the ground. The horse stood as if fettered.

"*Aiee*," exclaimed Black Otter. "He is tied to the sand! How did you do that?"

"I will show you," Horse Seeker smiled. "I first tied him to a boulder until he learned the word. It is 'stay' in my own tongue. Now when he hears it, he thinks he is tied."

"I must go back," Spotted Elk interrupted. "When you are ready, send Black Otter to tell me."

"It will be many days, Uncle. It is only the Moon of Roses."

"Yes, I know. But when he tells me, we will move the River People. Then you follow. Black Otter will come back to show you the way."

"It is good. I will see you at Medicine Rocks, my chief."

Spotted Elk turned and rode away.

"Now, Horse Seeker," began Black Otter, "how do I help you?"

"We have much to do, my friend. First the Dream-horse must know of other riders. Come, we will start."

Through the bright sunny days of the Moon of Roses the two worked with the horse. First it was a matter of merely riding together side by side. The red stallion became accustomed to another rider's presence at his shoulder. They moved at a walk, trot, and canter, gaining variety in experience.

As the training progressed, the two young men talked. They spoke of nothing in particular, sometimes loudly, sometimes softly. If the red stallion became uneasy, Horse Seeker was quick to reassure him with the soft tones of the medicine song.

Soon they could not only speak, but shout without bothering the Dream-horse whatever. Then, on an impulse, Horse Seeker decided to condition the animal also to the war cry of the People.

At a full gallop, he voiced for the first time in many moons the full-throated challenge that traditionally had taken generations of his tribe into battle. To his satisfaction, the stallion only flattened his ears and ran faster.

"*Aiee!*" chortled Black Otter. "That is your war cry? It makes my neck hair stand up!"

"That is its purpose," answered Horse Seeker, reining in beside his friend. "Now, come, we must learn the charge."

Again and again in the next days, they practiced running full at each other, passing the other animal so closely they brushed the legs of the riders. Next the process continued with both riders waving clubs, sticks, or branches, clashing the objects together as they passed In this way, the Dream-horse was introduced to the appearance of clashing weapons in combat.

Each charge was accompanied by the throaty war cry of the People. Black Otter, also, met each clash with yells and shouts. Soon the red stallion completely ignored all the new sights and sounds attending the mock combat.

There were long rides through the hills and among the scattered pines. Horse Seeker carried the lance. In a very short while, the Dream-horse accepted this as a normal daily routine.

He would stand ground-tied, held only by Horse Seeker's medicine. As a precaution, however, the horse was placed in the enclosure each night.

"We must find buffalo," Horse Seeker said one morning as they rose to greet the dawn. "The Dream-horse must learn the feel of the lance when it strikes.'

Already the horse was completely unmoved by any distraction they could contrive. He remained steady and confident in spite of whirling ropes carried by either man. Even the lance of Horse Seeker could be rested on the animal's withers or balanced across his back. Now it was time to teach the purpose of these things.

They found a small band of buffalo in a little pocket in the hills, ideal for their purpose.

"Ah, it is good," spoke Black Otter. "You can approach through the pines there."

The two skirted through the pines and circled to the north end of the basin, taking care to remain out of sight of the grazing buffalo. When they finally reached the point from which to launch the strike, they were not more than a hundred paces from the little herd.

They moved into the open at a walk, slowly at first, then increasing their speed to a trot.

The grazing buffalo raised their heads and began to shuffle away without alarm. Their concern increased as the intruders drew nearer. Concern led to alarm and finally panic as the herd bolted to escape.

Horse Seeker had selected a young cow. They could make use of fresh meat. The animal fled straightaway, running for the shelter of the wooded slope ahead.

From the beginning of the charge, the Dream-horse seemed to understand its purpose. Ears flattened, he leaped into a sprint which closed the space between the running animals.

Horse Seeker readied the lance as they approached on the left side of the galloping cow. With precision, the knife-sharp flint lance point pierced the soft flank of the quarry, ranging downward through heart and lungs.

Now, though the entire sequence took only the space of a heartbeat, timing was critical. The horse must stop quickly. If he continued his run, the lance might be twisted from the grasp of the hunter or even broken. Horse Seeker drew back on the rawhide rein, and the Dream-horse dropped his massive hindquarters to come to a sliding halt. The cow stumbled, falling forward as Horse Seeker withdrew the lance. The entire charge had been accomplished so smoothly that it was worthy of a buffalo horse of long experience.

Horse Seeker held the lance aloft, waving at his companion. He could not resist a yell of triumph as Black Otter rode to join him.

"Now, Otter! Now we are ready. Go and tell Spotted Elk!"

37

>> >> >>

Black Otter returned a day later, restless with excitement. Spotted Elk, he reported, would break camp the following day and start the move to the Medicine Rocks. There they would camp to await the arrival of Horse Seeker.

That event would be expected three days later. Horse Seeker had suggested that the combat take place with Sun Boy directly overhead to provide better use of light. This would eliminate the possibility of being caught at a disadvantage with the sun in his eyes.

Therefore, Spotted Elk would immediately, on arrival, announce to the Blue Paints that the young challenger would arrive at midday, three suns hence. This would begin the buildup of emotion, the songs and dancing, the celebration and excitement before the event.

Spotted Elk's plan included the attempt to raise a doubt, a little concern on the part of the Blue Paint chief. The River People would sing, dance, and celebrate through the night. Hopefully, this would make the Blue Paints suspicious, restless, and even sleepless.

Horse Seeker, meanwhile, would be traveling at a leisurely pace, resting well at night. Until his actual arrival, there would remain a certain doubt for the Blue Paint chief.

Black Otter related all these things, chuckling as he talked. His enthusiasm was easy to catch. Then he brought out his final surprise, a shapeless bundle, and handed it to Horse Seeker.

"Here. Bright Leaf says you must look like a chief."

Horse Seeker opened the bundle to find a new shirt and leggings. They were of finest white buckskin, heavily ornamented with quillwork. Beneath were new moccasins, also ornamented.

"*Aiee*, they are beautiful!"

He examined the intricate geometric designs.

"The patterns are those of my own people," he observed, astonished. "How . . . ?"

Black Otter was chuckling with delight.

"Yes," he nodded. "Bright Leaf took the designs from your old shirt. Here, try them on."

The garments fit perfectly. There was enough room in the shoulders for easy action. The footwear, though of a slightly different design than those of his own people, was comfortable.

"And here," Black Otter finished, "is your paint."

He handed a couple of small gourds containing pigments of red and yellow. Spotted Elk had thought of everything. The young warrior would enter combat in ceremonial dress and paint.

"Are the colors right?" Black Otter was asking. "Elk was not sure."

"Yes, it is good. I will use these and black from the fire. Otter, it is good."

There was time, now. They must wait before following the River People. The two young men talked, in the next few days, of many things. Black Otter voiced sympathetic concern for Yellow Bird.

"This makes my heart heavy, too, Otter. You know we wish to marry. But, she was alive when we saw her."

"You saw her? Spotted Elk did not tell me that."

"Yes. She is the prisoner of a young warrior. We hope that will protect her from the others."

He paused and gave a long sigh.

"But I may have to fight him next."

* * *

A day's journey away, Blue Jay was thinking remarkably similar thoughts. His concern had increased ever since the River People had arrived. There was something about their attitude that made him uncomfortable.

There was a confidence, somehow, that seemed out of place. Why should these people, of a lesser tribe, sing and celebrate? Their chanting and the sound of the dance drums lasted through each night until the dawn. It was beginning to bother him.

His prisoner, meanwhile, seemed relaxed and confident. It was as if the depressing sound of the drums each night had the opposite effect on her.

"Why do you smile?" he demanded angrily in sign talk. "Your lover will soon die. Are you eager for my bed?"

The girl smiled more broadly.

"Look at Walks-Like-Thunder," she suggested. "He is becoming weaker. The medicine of my warrior's people will kill him."

"No! It is not true," Blue Jay denied. "But even if it is, I would kill your lover. You will be my wife!"

He turned away in anger. From across the grassy basin, at the camp of the River People, came the sound of the incessant drums. It was infuriating.

He stalked through his own camp, angry and frustrated. Ahead, he saw Walks-Like-Thunder. The big man stood gazing into the distance as he listened to the drums of the River People. The chief, too, looked angry and frustrated.

Blue Jay hesitated to even speak, so dark was the expression on the chief's face. He could not completely avoid the meeting, so he merely nodded in recognition as he passed. Walks-Like-Thunder barely acknowledged the greeting.

Now Blue Jay truly began to wonder. Could it be true about the elk-dog medicine? Walks-Like-Thunder looked tired, concerned. Was the object around his neck really sucking the strength and manhood from the chief's body?

No, Blue Jay told himself. That was nonsense. The chief was only irritated by the constant beat of the drums across the meadow. Walks-Like-Thunder could not be defeated in combat. Certainly not by this slender youth,

no older than himself, on a borrowed horse. That one—
Blue Jay could not see why the girl would want him for a
lover. The man was thin, almost emaciated, ragged, and
dirty. Ah, there was no understanding the tastes of women.

But he, Blue Jay, would make her forget. She only
needed a night in the bed of a real man, a warrior of the
Blue Paints. And that would come soon.

Any way in which the fight ended, Blue Jay told himself, would be good for his purposes. If, as seemed likely,
the young stranger was killed, the girl would be his. But
what if, by some chance, the younger man succeeded in
defeating Walks-Like-Thunder? Blue Jay would have to
face him.

It would take some trick, some unknown medicine, to
defeat Thunder. This could also be dangerous to Blue Jay.
So it would be wise, he decided, to be prepared to strike
at once, before the young warrior had time to recover.

Yes, he must place himself in a position near the
meadow where the fight would take place. He would be
well armed but hidden. If Walks-Like-Thunder killed the
other, Blue Jay would do nothing.

But if the chief fell, Blue Jay would rush forward. His
people would be proud that he had brought vengeance. In
his mind, he saw the Blue Paint warriors rising to follow
his lead. They would overrun the detested River People,
killing and plundering. He, Blue Jay, would be the hero of
the day.

And, of course, the girl would be his. He smiled to
himself and strolled down to the meadow to find his
position, his place to wait during the fight.

38

» » »

The Medicine Rocks could be seen for a long distance. There were perhaps twenty or more in number, their yellow coloration distinguished from the reddish brown of the other formations. They stood stiffly, outlined against the green of the pines behind them. At certain times of the day, in changing light and shadow, the rocks seemed to march along the slope like determined warriors of a forgotten age of giants.

Some of the spires tapered to the upper end, like gnarled fingers thrust from beneath the earth's crust. A few of the taller shafts were capped by a flat crown of slightly different strata, gray in color. These larger columns took on the appearance of gigantic mushrooms, three times the height of a man.

It was thought that all the spires were once capped like those with the mushroom appearance. Piles of loose shale at their bases indicated that many winters of time had worn down the formations, constantly changing the shapes of the silent sentinels. In fact, within the memory of people now living, one of the great caps had fallen. It had

been considered an evil omen, and each misfortune for
several seasons had been attributed by some to this event.

The area had long been a meeting place for many
tribes. It was easily recognizable by description. There
was water, a reliable stream fed by melting ice in the
high country. There was adequate grass for the horses of
those camped in the area. The same features attracted
game.

Directly in front of the slope with the rock formations
was a level meadow. It was oval in shape, a long bow
shot wide and perhaps three in length. Here had been
held many races and contests, under the brooding presence of the Medicine Rocks sentinels on the slope above.
Today, they would bear witness to one more contest, a
fight to the death.

The River People were camped at the south end of the
arena, the Blue Paints at the north. Usually there would
be much interchange between tribes camped thus. There
would be trading of supplies, robes, and weapons. Some
would gamble with the sticks or the plum stones, and
there would be wagers on horse races or contests of skill.
Even traditional enemies engaged in such activities at
times like this.

However, there was very little such activity on this
occasion. There was too much distrust, too much dread
of the might of the Blue Paints under Walks-Like-Thunder.

The River People, though not mixing with the others,
had continued their celebration since their arrival. It was
becoming increasingly annoying to the Blue Paints, the
incessant thump of the drums, the high-pitched singing
and chanting.

In the meadow, some of the young men of both tribes
rode horses, sprinting, shouting, waving weapons aloft in
boasting show of ferocity. Both groups knew there would
be no conflict. It was simply a good chance to brag and
threaten, to flaunt manhood. There were many derisive
shouts, threats, and taunts in the sign talk and much
obscene gesturing.

As midday approached, people began to drift toward
the meadow. Choice seats were quickly taken, and before long each rock in the vicinity of the meadow held its
limit of observers.

Walks-Like-Thunder entered the meadow from his

camp. He was dressed and painted for battle and carried
only his massive war axe and a rawhide shield. He was
mounted on a trim gray mare, who danced nervously,
sensing action ahead.

Almost instantly, the arena emptied of young horsemen.
No one of either tribe cared to share the attention of the
crowd with such a warrior. The Blue Paint chief jogged
easily around the meadow, strutting and swinging his
great stone axe, singing and shouting what appeared to
be threats.

He completed a circuit of the arena, swinging toward
the center only once. A clutter of boulders and broken
stone thrust into the west side of the oval, breaking the
symmetry of form. It was this area that the rider avoided.
There was enough room elsewhere for maneuvering or
fighting.

On the next circuit, Walks-Like-Thunder began to chide
the River People along the edge of the meadow. He had
handed his weapon and shield to someone and now used
both hands to deride in sign talk as he rode.

"Where is your warrior? Hiding with the women? I
was to kill him today!"

He reached the south end of the circle and stopped
before Spotted Elk.

"I see no warrior. Where has he hidden? Who will fight
me now? You, Spotted Elk?"

It was an unfair challenge. Spotted Elk, though a capable leader, was past his prime as a warrior. It was an
obvious insult, designed to goad some of the younger
warriors into unwise action. Spotted Elk remained calm.

"Horse Seeker will be here."

"Horse Seeker? Why does he seek a horse? I have
found his horse." He pointed to the mount under him.
"He must only claim it! Where is Horse Seeker?"

No one moved as the Blue Paint rode along the edge of
the crowd challenging individuals to fight. It appeared
that his temper was growing short.

Spotted Elk was becoming concerned. He had no doubt
that Horse Seeker would appear. His concern was whether
Walks-Like-Thunder would create an incident before that
time. Any overt act could start the outbreak of a general
melee, in which the River People would be outnumbered
by two to one.

For the first time, Spotted Elk began to doubt. Perhaps the entire scheme was unwise. Regardless of the outcome of this fight, the Blue Paints might attack and overrun his people's camp. They were known for their treachery. Well, it was too late now.

A commotion made him turn. Two riders were approaching around the shoulder of the hill.

A sound began among the River People, a sort of gasp of pleased astonishment at first. It grew, spreading like ripples on a still pond, becoming louder as it spread. Quickly it became a cheer, a tumult of sound that echoed across the valley.

"It is Horse Seeker!"

"The Fire-horse! He rides the Fire-horse!"

"Never was there such medicine!"

The River People were jumping, dancing, shouting, and singing now before the astonished eyes of Walks-Like-Thunder.

Horse Seeker kneed the great red stallion forward, the crowd parting before him. He saw that Walks-Like-Thunder was unarmed, so he handed his lance to Black Otter. He could use both hands for sign talk.

He quickly saw that the Blue Paint was mounted on the stolen mare, Gray Cloud. It was also painfully obvious that the Spanish bit dangled on its thong around the man's neck. It glittered in the sunlight as it swung gently with the motion of the nervous horse.

Now was the time, Horse Seeker knew, to retain the initiative. The Blue Paint was still in a state of surprised shock. He urged the Dream-horse forward until they stood practically touching the nervous Gray Cloud. Horse Seeker had been searching for a phrase in sign talk which would so infuriate the big man that his judgment would be impaired.

"Fat man," he signed, "your mother eats dung!"

39

>> >> >>

Livid with rage, Walks-Like-Thunder jerked the gray's head around and sprinted toward the other end of the arena for his weapons. Horse Seeker took his lance from Black Otter and moved forward at a slow walk. Let the other come to him. Let him tire the gray horse by loping unnecessarily.

He had not long to wait. The Blue Paint came charging back across the meadow, a heavy shield on his left arm and the stone axe making whistling noises at each circle through the air. It was a fearsome thing to see. Horse Seeker was pleased that his mount stood still, only shifting slightly in anticipation.

"Now, my brother," he whispered in the animal's ear, "the time has come. Remember our medicine."

He nudged the glossy flanks with both heels, at the same time splitting the air with the full-throated war cry of the People. This the horse understood. Great muscles bunched and drove the stallion forward, at top speed in a few jumps. Horse Seeker gripped the lance, lowered its point, and aimed straight at the bare midriff of the approaching Blue Paint.

The lance point was aimed true, but the skill and experience of the other warrior came into play. At the last moment, Walks-Like-Thunder swung his heavy shield to parry the thrust. The shock nearly tore the lance from Horse Seeker's grasp, but he maintained his balance and the two horses swept on past each other. At least the Blue Paint had not managed to bring the axe into play.

Now Horse Seeker realized that he was in trouble. It had appeared so easy, the other's use of the thick bull-hide shield. It would be very difficult to use the lance.

One common alternative in such a case would be to kill the opponent's horse, placing him on foot. Could he bring himself to kill the gray mare, finest of his tribe's stock, to save himself and the battle? He had only a moment to decide. The Blue Paint had wheeled and was thundering down on him again.

Horse Seeker lowered the lance point, his attention on the crescent-shaped line where the mare's neck met the bulging muscles of her chest. He saw that she was breathing hard, winded from the relentless push of her rider.

Now it would be necessary to strike and immediately dodge the swing of the axe as they swept past.

His resolve, so firm as they started the run, wavered at the last moment. He could not do it. The lance point jerked upward, and he reined the confused Dream-horse aside to avoid the clash.

They almost escaped unscathed. Almost. The stone axe of the Blue Paint, who was swinging blindly at arm's reach, chanced to encounter the lance shaft just behind the head. The shock of the impact numbed Horse Seeker's right arm and tore the shattered weapon from his hand.

Frantically, he fumbled at his waist for the small axe, desperate now. He turned to see the Blue Paint start forward again, the swiging club readied for its final arc. Gray Cloud was wheezing now, reeling from exhaustion. If the Dream-horse could outmaneuver the other, approaching from the opponent's left side, they could avoid the wicked swing of the great war axe. Even Walks-Like-Thunder could not make an efficient swing to his left with the club in his right hand.

The stallion sprang forward at command, circling the other animal. Of course, this also made Horse Seeker's weapon practically useless against the shield on the opponent's left arm. But that was not his purpose.

The Blue Paint pushed the horse forward, thrusting his bulk against the tired mare, continuing to push. The mare sidestepped, missed her footing, and fell heavily on her side.

Walks-Like-Thunder rolled free but had not yet recovered from the fall when his opponent landed on his back. Horse Seeker realized that he must not allow the other to regain his feet. There would be no chance at all against the massive swing of the Blue Paint's weapon. They rolled in the dust, over and over, Horse Seeker clawing, grasping, sticking to the big man's shoulders like a bur in a buffalo's shaggy coat. Walks-Like-Thunder could not reach behind to bring a weapon into play. He attempted to rise to his knees.

Horse Seeker was tiring. The arm encircling the other's neck was losing its grasp. Frantically, he grasped at anything to hold, and his fingers closed on a rawhide thong. He pulled, and a choked sound told him that this was the thong which encircled the Blue Paint's neck, holding the elk-dog medicine. He continued to pull with all his strength. The Blue Paint was on his knees, now, grasping at the metal which crushed against his windpipe.

Horse Seeker was not certain his strength would last. Then he saw, on the ground where it had fallen, the broken lance shaft. This was the forward portion, with the sharp flint point. If he could only reach it. He stretched as far as he could without releasing his twisting grip on the other's neck. Ah, there! He grasped the broken weapon.

To his dismay, the flint point was shattered, useless. He had only a slender staff not as long as his arm. Desperately, he thrust the stick through the loop of the thong behind the neck of his opponent. He began to twist.

Walks-Like-Thunder's eyes bulged; his face mottled and darkened. Horse Seeker could feel, rather than hear, the cracking and crushing of the metal bit against the cartilages of the big man's neck.

Walks-Like-Thunder tottered like a falling tree and plunged forward on his face in the dust.

Exhausted, hardly able to stand, Horse Seeker dropped

to his knees to remove the elk-dog medicine from the neck of his enemy.

"I told you," he muttered to the still form, "that my medicine would kill you."

A few steps away the Dream-horse stood, ground-tied. The animal did not understand all that had happened. There was much noise and confusion. He could see the man who had become his brother bending over the still form on the ground. It was apparent that there had been danger here.

Now, from the edge of his vision, he sensed another danger. In a clutter of jumbled rocks which jutted into the meadow was a stealthy movement. Memories came creeping back into the brain of the horse. This was like the threat of the cougar creeping upon an unsuspecting foal. Yet this was different, somehow. This creeping thing should have been walking erect, on two legs.

Still, the danger was there. The prey of the stalker was obviously the unsuspecting man bending over the other. Conflicting thoughts whirled in the brain of the stallion. He must not move when the rein was dropped like this. But instinct told him to protect the man who had become part of the herd and now was his brother. The horse fidgeted nervously.

The creeping figure rose and rushed forward, weapon upraised over the back of the helpless Horse Seeker.

The stallion screamed in rage and rushed forward as he had at the cougar long before. Blue Jay turned in surprise but had time for only one choked scream before the flint-hard hooves struck.

Horse Seeker turned, startled, in time to see the great red form rear high into the air, striking down, again and again, flashing hooves pounding the already lifeless form into the dust.

Beyond, through the dust of the conflict, he saw people running toward him. First to reach him was Yellow Bird.

40

>> >> >>

The dust of battle had hardly settled down when the first of the lodges came down in the Blue Paint camp. The wail of their Mourning Song echoed across the meadow. The River People withdrew to allow the other tribe to claim their dead.

There was no attempt to continue hostilities. It was plain that the Blue Paints, who had seen the power of the stranger's medicine, wanted no more demonstrations. They were leaving.

Never had Horse Seeker seen an encampment empty so quickly. Long before the shadows lengthened, the defeated Blue Paints were represented only by a fading puff of dust in the distance.

Now fires were lighted, and celebration began in earnest. Dance after dance reenacted the great triumphs, the death of Yellow Bird's captor by the hooves of the Firehorse, Horse Seeker's victory over the enemy chief, and all other triumphs of the River People since memory began.

Children at play enacted the spectacular scene with

the great red horse crushing the life from Horse Seeker's unseen attacker.

The Dream-horse had been removed to a quiet place to avoid the excitement of so many people. Horse Seeker spent a little while alone with the animal, talking and calming his excitement. He had only to explain to the people that this was part of his medicine. The horse must now be left alone. He tied the animal securely and rejoined Yellow Bird and the others.

"You will stay with us now?" Bright Leaf asked hopefully.

Horse Seeker shook his head.

"No, I must go to my own people. I must take this," he pointed to the shiny elk-dog medicine on his chest, "and I must help my father as medicine man."

Reluctantly, the River People accepted this. Still, it was with great honor that the marriage of Horse Seeker and Yellow Bird was carried out. When the girl's father finally drew the robe around the shoulders of the couple to symbolize his approval of the union, there were no two happier people alive.

Several suns later, the young couple sat contentedly watching the shadows grow long. Their campfire flickered cheerfully.

They had crossed the dangerous Sand Hills and were now in more hospitable country. Grass grew thick and green ahead of them. A few steps away, the Dream-horse grazed quietly, tethered by a long rope. The girl's spotted mare, Gray Cloud, and the black mare followed closely. Horse Seeker had taken the precaution of tying the stallion each night, though the animal had made no attempt to escape.

Now the two watched as the Dream-horse raised his head to look far across the prairie. In the distance, a band of wild horses could be seen along a low ridge. The stallion called, a long, trumpeting whinny, but the horses were too far away to hear.

A lone crow swooped low, making its way toward a fringe of willow in the distance. The bird uttered three hoarse cries, and Yellow Bird was sure that the crow cocked its head to look at her husband.

Horse Seeker rose, hobbled the three mares, and then

approached the Dream-horse. He led the horse a few steps into the prairie and slipped the rope from his head.

"Thank you, my brother," he whispered.

The horse stood for only a moment. Then he lunged away, running at top speed, without a backward look. Horse Seeker coiled his rope and walked slowly back to the fire.

"You have freed the Dream-horse?" the girl asked in astonishment.

"Yes." He came and sat beside her. "I asked him to help me only for a little while."

Yellow Bird smiled and leaned her head on his shoulder.

"That is part of your medicine?"

He circled her with an arm.

"Yes, little one. Another part is this: our three mares carry the seed of the Dream-horse. We will have the finest herd ever seen."

She snuggled in the crook of his arm and smiled contentedly. Her medicine was also good.

GENEALOGY

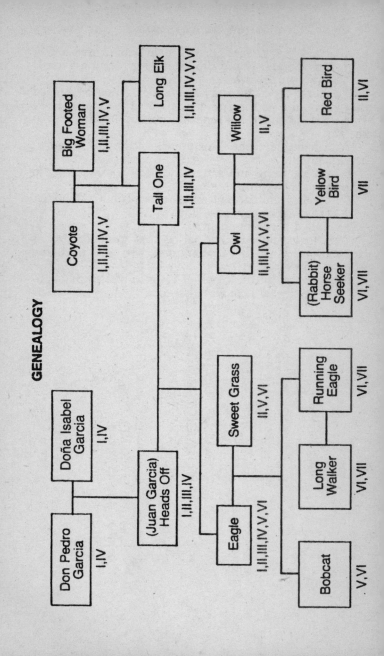

Dates for Volumes in the Spanish Bit Saga

I   TRAIL OF THE SPANISH BIT — 1540-44
II   BUFFALO MEDICINE   — 1559-61
III THE ELK-DOG HERITAGE   — 1544-45
IV FOLLOW THE WIND   — 1547-48
V   MAN OF THE SHADOWS   — 1565-66
VI DAUGHTER OF THE EAGLE — 1583-84
VII MOON OF THUNDER   — 1600-01

Dates are only approximate, since the People have no written calendar.

Volume II, BUFFALO MEDICINE, is out of chronological order, and should appear between Volumes IV and V.

Characters in the Genealogy appear in the volumes indicated.

ABOUT THE AUTHOR

DON COLDSMITH is a physician who lives in Emporia, Kansas. In addition to his Spanish Bit novels, he writes a syndicated newspaper column on horses. He is himself a breeder of Appaloosas. Mr. Coldsmith is a past president of the Western Writers of America.

So far, seven novels in the Spanish Bit Saga have been published as Double D Westerns: *Trail of the Spanish Bit, Buffalo Medicine, The Elk-dog Heritage, Follow the Wind, Man of the Shadows, Daughter of the Eagle,* and *Moon of Thunder.*

A Proud People In a Harsh Land

THE SPANISH BIT SAGA

Set on the Great Plains of America in the early 16th century, Don Coldsmith's acclaimed series recreates a time, a place and a people that have been nearly lost to history. With the advent of the Spaniards, the horse culture came to the people of the Plains. In THE SPANISH BIT SAGA we see history in the making through the eyes of the proud Native Americans who lived it.

THE SPANISH BIT SAGA
Don Coldsmith

- ☐ BOOK 1: TRAIL OF THE SPANISH BIT   26397 $2.95
- ☐ BOOK 2: THE ELK-DOG HERITAGE   26412 $2.95
- ☐ BOOK 3: FOLLOW THE WIND   26806 $2.95
- ☐ BOOK 4: BUFFALO MEDICINE   26938 $2.95
- ☐ BOOK 5: MAN OF THE SHADOWS   27067 $2.95
- ☐ BOOK 6: DAUGHTER OF THE EAGLE   27209 $2.95
- ☐ BOOK 7: MOON OF THUNDER   27344 $2.95
- ☐ BOOK 8: THE SACRED HILLS   27460 $2.95